P9-CDJ-474

ITCH

BY POLLY FARQUHAR

HOLIDAY HOUSE ❖ NEW YORK

HOLIDAY HOUSE is registered in the U.S. Patent and Trademark Office.
Printed and bound in December 2019 at Maple Press, York, PA, USA.
www.holidayhouse.com
First Edition
1 3 5 7 9 10 8 6 4 2

Library of Congress Cataloging-in-Publication Data

Names: Farquhar, Polly, author.
Title: Itch / by Polly Farquhar.
Description: First edition. | New York : Holiday House, [2020] | Audience:
Ages 8–12 | Audience: Grades 4–6 | Summary: Ohio sixth-grader Isaac
"Itch" Fitch strives to fit in, but everything seems to be going wrong, even
before a school lunch trade sends his best friend, Sydney, to the hospital.
Identifiers: LCCN 2019022610 | ISBN 9780823445523 (hardcover)
ISBN 9780823446346 (epub)
Subjects: CYAC: Friendship—Fiction. | Middle schools—Fiction.
Schools—Fiction. | Food allergy—Fiction. | Itching—Fiction. | Family
life—Ohio—Fiction. | Ohio—Fiction.
Classification: LCC PZ7.1.F3676 Itc 2020 | DDC [Fic]—dc23
LC record available at https://lccn.loc.gov/2019022610

ISBN: 978-0-8234-4552-3 (hardcover)

For my daughters

CHAPTER 1

THE DAY THE tornado came through, Sydney, Nate, and I were out riding our bikes together, burning down the banks of the river and then splashing into the water. The river was wide, slow, and muddy. The grass in the yards had turned a crunchy kind of yellow and the corn in the field that stood between us and the gas station was taller than even Nate. It was August. School started next week. Sixth grade.

Up at the top of the riverbank, Sydney rocked back and forth on her bike. "Ready?"

Nate already stood in the river with his bike, the water up to the middle of the wheels. The water was low because it had been dry, which was good because when there was a lot of rain the river turned green and stuff grew on it. From farm runoff, my dad said.

Nate yelled, "Go! Go! Go!"

Sydney skidded down the steep bank—the closest thing to a hill around here—fighting with her handlebars as she tried to keep control through the mud. Her bike sent up a big spray as it hit the shallow water, and she shrieked. I followed her down and mud splattered all the way up to my face, and then the splash of water soaked my shirt. The day was the kind of hot that felt like it was sitting on you. The water wasn't much cooler, but at least it was wet. I didn't even think about itching.

As we hauled our bikes up to go again, Sydney said, "I can't believe school starts next week."

"Me neither," I said.

"At least football is starting up," Nate said. He chucked a clump of mud at me, but it went wide and splattered on Sydney's arm instead. The handful of mud I threw at Nate missed him completely.

Sydney laughed. "You guys will never play ball with arms like that."

"Watch me," Nate said, and he hit my leg on his next throw.

It had been a good summer.

Sydney lived down the street from me and we'd been friends since I first moved to Ohio. We hung out a lot— riding bikes on the riverbank, playing video games and then cards on the front porch when her parents kicked us out of the house, striking at her brothers with water balloons when they were doing yard work. Usually it was just the two of us. Then Nate started showing up with his bike at the river. And sometimes when I was hanging out with Nate, we hung out with the other guys from school.

Nate popped up the front wheel of his bike, tipping his head back to look at the sky, which was as dark as a bruise. "Let's go get slushies before it rains."

At the gas station, we tracked in mud. "We're swamp creatures," Sydney said. She pushed back her hair with her muddy arm. It was coming out of her braid and fuzzed all around her face.

There weren't any cars at the gas pumps. The day the tornado came through was also the first day of the Buckeye football preseason and the store was empty.

"Shoot," Sydney said, heading to the counter. "The slushie machine is broken." She looked at the guy at the cash register. "For real? That's all I want. That's all I want in the whole world. A slushie."

"There's ice cream in the back freezer."

"I only do the slushies. Thanks anyway."

I asked the guy if there had been any weather alerts, but he said he'd only been listening to the game. "Buckeyes up by fourteen already," he told us. That's how it is in Ohio. Everybody is always talking Ohio State University football.

"It's going to be a blowout," Nate said, cracking

his knuckles, and I guess Nate knew the guy because they started talking about the game and then Nate's grandparents.

"Excuse me," I said, butting in, "but are you sure there isn't even a watch out? Or a thunderstorm warning?"

All spring there had been tornadoes, the kind that busted out of the sky in the middle of the night. Invisible demons in the dark, roaring as they came to eat you, your house, your town. It got so bad everywhere that my grandmother, who lived in another state, followed our weather. Sometimes she called us before our town's tornado sirens even went off. She called if it was the middle of the night. The weather was so bad that no one minded. The wail of tornado sirens is hard to hear when you're inside a house, asleep, with the air conditioner running.

"Maybe," the guy said. "Sorry about the slushies."

Nate said, "We can find something at my grandmother's."

We rode our bikes farther down the empty roads to Nate's grandmother's storage units—the Storage-U—and she had Popsicles in the freezer in her office. They were the kind in plastic tubes that you freeze at home. Sydney read the ingredients on the box. Big blue clouds rolled in, fat and heavy.

It felt like *before*.

We ate fast.

The Storage-U was three long lines of cinder block buildings with red metal doors and three long gravel driveways. The office was a trailer near the road. Nate's grandmother was working inside. After a while, she banged on the window and waved us away, and I shoved the empty Popsicle wrapper into my pocket and climbed on my bike.

"Go Bucks!" Nate, his teeth still around the plastic tube, peeled off toward his house with a wave, but I lived farther on, and Sydney a block beyond me. It was hot and soupy, but the wind that pushed in was cold.

Once Sydney and I made it to our street, it took us three minutes to get to my house. I knew that because the tornado sirens started to wail, and they wail solid for three minutes before turning off and then starting up again.

The sirens are loud. Piercing. The sound goes right through your body and down into your soul and rattles your earwax.

My mother stood out on the steps of our front porch. My mom is neat and orderly, but right then she looked wild, with the wind blowing her hair so it covered her face. She yelled into the phone. "They're here! She's here. I've got them. I'll get her into our basement."

She stopped us from hauling our bikes up onto the front porch and we left them clattering down to the sidewalk behind us. We kept on our helmets and wet shoes. In the living room, the Buckeyes played silently in a little rectangle in the corner of the television. The rest of the picture was nothing but weather guys. Let me tell you this: no one interrupts the Buckeyes. If the Buckeyes are silent, it can only be a matter of life or death. "If you live in the warning box on the map," the weather guy said, "you need to take shelter now."

In the basement, my mom handed Sydney the phone and told her to call her parents. "Just so they know you're here and safe. It was wild out there. They might not have heard me." Mom turned on the weather radio. Dad was at work even though it was a Saturday. We sat in old lawn chairs. The futon was covered with suitcases.

Sydney asked, "What's with all the suitcases? Are you going somewhere?"

"Mom's going to China."

"For real?" She looked at all the suitcases again. "Is she *moving* there?"

"It's a business trip."

"I leave next week," Mom said. "I'm still trying to evaluate the best suitcase."

"Wow, China. That's awesome."

Mom didn't even know how long she would be gone. She said at least two months. There wasn't anything awesome about it.

Mom offered us snacks. "We've got some stashed down here for occasions just like this." She got some candy from a grocery bag hanging on an old coat tree.

"Mom! Come on. You can't give Sydney that stuff." I said it the same time Sydney said no, thank you. Polite. The way she always speaks to grown-ups. She's so good at it my mother tells me I should talk like her.

Mom stuck the miniature candy bars in her pocket and I ran up the stairs where it was loud with rain and sirens and grabbed a bag of pretzels that was a brand I knew Sydney could eat and a two-liter bottle of root beer. Back down in the basement I asked her, "This okay?"

"Yeah," Sydney said, taking the pretzels from me. "Thanks."

Hail hit the small basement windows and the wind hollered. The lights browned out and then were gone, and it was just us, the storm that sounded like a military plane with its belly scraping over the roof of our house, and the weather radio.

Then it was *after.*

The street was filled with garbage and trash can lids and roof shingles and tree branches and lawn chairs. A couple of trees were down. My bike lay in the middle of the road. Sydney's was just gone. Downed power lines lay across the sidewalk like giant black snakes. They hissed like snakes too.

Mom stopped us right on the front porch, her hands clutching tightly into my shoulder. She grabbed Sydney too.

"Not one step more. Those are live power lines. We're not going anywhere near them. Let's try heading out through the backyard."

So that's how we went, through the wet grass and through neighbors' yards and across the street to Sydney's house, where one of her older brothers, Dylan, came running toward us. He was yelling about Sydney's bike.

"It's in a tree! We found it in a tree! Come and see!"

The bike was caught in an oak tree one house down from Sydney's. It's a giant tree. Her bike hung up as high as the second story. "I wonder if I can see it from my bedroom," she said as we stood looking up at it. The bike hung from its back wheel, twigs and branches and leaves all jammed through its spokes.

"Wow, Isaac," she said, her head still tipped up, "you saved my life."

"It was mostly my mom." Some of the smaller branches creaked under the bike's weight, and we hustled back.

"Still, though. Thanks," she said, her eyes on the tree.

"Anytime."

Mom said, "Let's just hope it won't have to happen too often."

"I can totally agree with that." Then Sydney hugged

Mom and told her to have a good trip to China. She cut away from the tree and through her grass to her brother, and Mom and I went home through backyards again.

That night it was dark and hot and quiet and there were more stars in the sky than I had ever seen in my life. We sat out on the front porch. Mom and Dad sat in the rocking chairs but didn't rock and I sat on the top porch step and looked up at the sky until my neck ached, and when I finally looked away all I saw were pricks of starlight.

I asked Mom, "Will you see the same stars over China that we do in Ohio?"

Mom said she didn't know for sure. "I'm going to be a little farther south, so that changes some of the stars I might see. We'll be in the same hemisphere," she said, "so maybe it won't be too different."

"You should be sure to remember to take a look," Dad said, "for scientific purposes."

Would a person even notice if the stars in the sky were different? Even if you'd never thought about the stars or the sky or constellations before and if you were far away from home, would you be able to look up to a different night sky and see that it wasn't the same as yours? Would you know right away? Maybe it would be the kind of thing that even though you'd never thought about it, you'd recognize it right away, like how toilets flush the other way in Australia. You'd notice that, right, if you were visiting Australia? But what if you didn't notice? What if everything was different and you didn't even know?

The rocking chair rocked once as Mom got off and came to sit with me on the step. She looked up at the sky with me. It's a big sky right here in Ohio. There's nothing that gets in the way of it.

Mom told me to look at the moon. A hazy white hook of a moon sat in the sky above the oak tree that had caught Sydney's bike. "The moon will be the same."

CHAPTER 2

*T*HE TORNADO PEELED away the school's cafeteria roof like an old Band-Aid and blew out walls, turning the rain into solid bricks. Debris beat up fields of feed corn and soybeans and busted cars and killed a couple of pigs out at Tyler's dad's pig farm. Some of Nate's grandmother's storage units were blown apart. Nate said every now and then someone called saying they found a chair or a table or a grill out in a field, wondering if maybe it was from their place.

Sydney's dad got her bike down from the tree. She said her handlebars were wonky and the wheels were bent and her dad was going to try to fix it, but she wasn't in a hurry because she liked the proof of what happened, of us out-biking the tornado and then her bike stuck up in a tree.

We lost power for a couple of days after the storm and it was hot, so I started sleeping in the basement. Once the power came back on I didn't bother going back up.

The basement is peaceful. It has three high, rectangular

windows, and when the sun shines through late in the morning it's almost as bright as any room upstairs. There's just a radio and the futon (which is actually really comfortable) and some old lawn furniture and an old TV that no one ever bothered to plug in. I added a clothes basket of clothes and my computer.

When the power came back on, Mom said she thought I should go back upstairs to my bedroom. "How long are you staying down there?"

"I don't know. I like it. It's cooler than the rest of the house."

Two days before school started we drove Mom to the airport. We waited around with her until we had to say goodbye at security. "I can't believe it," she said, slinging her arm around my shoulders. "Look at you, getting so tall."

"I can't believe you're going to China." I didn't know anyone who went to China. Kids went to Disney and amusement parks and on cruises, but no one went to China.

"Me neither, kid," she said, shaking her head. "Remember when we moved out here? To Ohio?"

"Yeah." Of course I did. Three years ago Mom and I drove out in one car, Dad in the other, and even though I always sat in the back seat because that's where kids are supposed to sit, Mom let me move up to the front so I could pass her snacks and help her with the GPS and read signs. Every time we crossed a state line it was a race to see who could touch the windshield first. I won two out of three, but only because I wasn't driving.

"I couldn't imagine living in Ohio either, then, but here we are. I'm sure I'll figure it out. One foot in front of the other."

I had her laptop bag over my shoulder. I started to itch my neck, under the strap. Mom grabbed my hand and tucked it into a fist.

"Stop," she said. Then she went through her list for me. Again. She'd been doing it all day. "Remember your medicine. Keep your grades up. Wear your helmet when you ride your bike. We'll video chat, okay?" She smiled. "And maybe don't go so far from home when storms are coming in. I think you took ten years off my life."

"I did not."

"You did. Trust me. Leaving you now is way easier than when I was looking for you and Sydney to finally come down the street."

Then it was hugs, and Mom and Dad kissed, and Mom said, "Take care of each other, okay?" and she headed through the metal detector. Dad and I got soft pretzels and sat by a window and waited for Mom to text us that she was boarding. We watched other planes take off. I pretended each one was hers. It was night and the planes were silver in the city's lights. They aimed up at the dark sky and then they were faraway blinking lights and then gone and they might as well have been stars.

She was flying to San Francisco and then Japan and then China. I pictured it like a cartoon, with the earth spinning one way and the plane going the other.

When we got home it was late, and Dad and I were hungry and we made fat peanut butter sandwiches. I stuffed chocolate chips in mine. We drank root beer. My teeth felt fuzzy from the sugar. The only light in the whole house was the yellow light above the sink. The world felt very small, just me and my dad.

Between bites, Dad said we should do something awesome, just the two of us. "Paint the living room. Or learn how to cook something really complicated."

"I'm not sure either of those ideas is very awesome."

"Right. Okay. Sure."

"For an old man, maybe."

He punched my shoulder. "Maybe one of those really complicated Lego sets?"

I shrugged.

"What do you think?" He took a bite of sandwich. The whole kitchen smelled like root beer and peanut butter.

I didn't have any bright ideas. I didn't ask about football. That didn't even start at school until seventh grade, and I knew my parents would never pay to sign me up for any of the leagues run by the parks department. So I just took a bite of sandwich. It wasn't as good as you'd think it would be, cold chocolate chips and soft sandwich bread.

CHAPTER 3

*T*HE SCHOOL'S CAFETERIA was gone but somehow we still had the gym. How could a tornado miss the gym? It was twice the height of the rest of the school and the tallest building around for miles, if you don't count the silos. Our gym teacher, Mr. Mullins, thought it was a miracle.

"How about it, boys? We're playing kickball today! Do you know what you'd be doing if we'd lost our beautiful gymnasium?"

Nate yelled, "Rock climbing!"

Mr. Mullins pointed at him and yelled right back. "More like hard labor with the janitors!"

"Rock climbing on what rocks?" That was Tyler. We stood around, waiting for Mr. Mullins to blow his whistle and send us off on our warm-up laps. Me, Nate, Daniel, Tyler, and Lucas. And the new kid. It was his first day of school, ever.

Behind me, Lucas whispered, "Like we couldn't just play kickball outside?"

Daniel said, "Who needs rocks? We could just climb a building."

"Yeah! Daniel's right," Nate said. "We could climb up to the second floor. Just climb up the bricks." He grinned. "Then climb in the windows."

That's when the new kid said, "It's called buildering."

We all swung our heads around to look at him. No one said anything. The new kid didn't notice. He kept talking. "Not the climbing in windows part, but the building-climbing part. It's *building* as in, you know, a building"—he waved around at the gym—"and then making it into a verb. It's also like bouldering, which is climbing boulders." He shrugged. "Self-explanatory."

I used to be the new kid. I wasn't born here. I'm not from Ohio. That matters to people. That's why when everybody else was silently staring at the *new* new kid, I said, "Oh. Okay."

He'd introduced himself to the class that morning. Popped right up from his chair and smiled and talked about himself as though he was sure we were all really interested in what he had to say. He'd been homeschooled. He was so happy about his first day of school—*ever*—he smiled the whole time. He'd told us about his summer vacation at the beach. He had food allergies, just like Sydney, and he told us about the foods he couldn't eat—nuts and some other things—and he pointed out the two EpiPens in a red case he had clipped to his pants pocket. "EpiPens are emergency epinephrine auto-injectors," he'd said, "and I don't go anywhere without them."

Tyler made his sneakers squeak over the gym floor and asked the new kid, "Do you do it? Climb buildings like that?"

Nate said, "That's pretty cool, Homeschool." Nate elbowed me. "Right, Itch?"

That's me. I'm Itch.

The new kid said no, he didn't climb buildings.

Mr. Mullins started up the automatic partition that divided the gym in half. It was motorized and unfolded by itself like someone was smoothing out a piece of folded paper. The girls were on the other side. Sydney waved to me, leaning sideways as the wall crept past her. I waved back. The girls' gym teacher was pretty new so they never got to play kickball. They measured pulses and heart rates and heart-rate intervals and calculated maximum results, or something, and jumped a lot, which Sydney told us was supposed to strengthen their bones.

Nate ran past me. He was big—the biggest kid in the

sixth grade, tall and solid—but slow. He didn't like being the last one done, so he always started his warm-up laps early. After we ran our laps we played kickball in half the gym. Even though it was way bigger than playing ball in one of Nate's grandmother's storage units, that's what it reminded me of. Except the gym had a lot of bright lights, and the storage units only had the light that came in through the open doors.

"This is dangerous," Nate said loudly. "Half the gym isn't enough room for a game."

Tyler said, "I don't think it's any more dangerous than climbing up the walls of the school," and Daniel said, "I think you mean bouldering."

Lucas said, "It's buildering. Because it's a school, not a rock."

"Right," Daniel said. "It's self-explanatory."

Tyler said, "Maybe it should be called schoolering."

This time, the new kid didn't say anything. Maybe it's the kind of thing you can figure out right away. You don't need all the school years leading up to it to know, right now, that these guys were not impressed to have some new vocabulary.

Dangerous or not, kickball in a box (that's what Nate called it) was fun. The red rubber ball got kicked and whipped hard. It burned your face and slapped your hands.

Because we played it in half the gym, it was part kickball and part dodgeball.

The new kid had second base. He hopped around on his toes, waiting. I was on first. Daniel and Tyler had pitcher and third. Nate was on the other team, and he was up.

Nate kicked. *Pow. Bam.* Hard, straight to second base. Daniel ducked out of pure self-defense. The ball shot past Daniel and right at the new kid.

I thought he was a goner. He was skinny. All head, elbows, and knees. It wasn't just that he had no fat, it didn't look he had any muscle either, only what it took to move his arms or walk and even that didn't look like much. He'd never had gym class before. Sure, maybe he'd played on kiddie teams, but he didn't have a lifetime of gym class experience. But then it turned into one of those gym class moments, the kind you remember forever. He snagged the ball out of the air and whipped it at Nate and dropped him. *Boom.* Nate flat-out hit the floor. Nate looked like he had just relaxed—as though he'd flung out his arms and was going to flop into a hammock but instead hit the wood of the gym floor.

For a minute, we just stared.

And that's when it happened to the new new kid. No one knew what to call him. We hadn't bothered to remember his name. We'd only been in school for two hours. We just had the thing Nate had said—Pretty cool, Homeschool. So when Daniel started yelling, that's what he was calling him. Sort of. Not Homeschool, though. He made it worse.

"Homer! Homer! Give him your shot! Where's your shot?" Sweat dripped down Daniel's face. "Come on!"

"It's not for that," Homer answered. "It's not for getting conked in the head."

"But-But-But—look at him!"

"Come on, give him the shot!" Some of the other boys joined in.

"It's a head injury," Tyler said. "Like with football or whatever on TV. He's unconscious. It's not from food. Obviously."

Daniel looked at Homer, hard. It was a staring contest, and Homer won because Daniel had to wipe the sweat off his forehead. His scalp, as pink as a hot dog, showed through his buzz cut. "Can't believe it, man."

Homer wiped his own sweat. "He doesn't need epinephrine."

By then Mr. Mullins was crouching down next to Nate. Nate's one of those kids who always has to be moving. I bet he can't even sleep lying down. It was weird to watch him lying so still on the shiny gym floor. Mr. Mullins watched Nate breathe for a second or two and then touched his shoulders. Nate blinked and scrambled to sit up. The worst thing about all this for Nate, I figured, was not losing consciousness or being taken out by Homeschool Homer, but being nudged awake by the gym teacher.

Homer asked me, "What if Daniel was right? What if my medicine could have helped Nate? Maybe it would." He rubbed his face with the collar of his sweaty T-shirt. "What if there is an off-label usage of which I am unaware? Besides, I really don't know anything about head injuries."

That's when I first noticed how he talked, like an essay the teacher would read aloud to the class as a good example.

I said, "But no one does that. At a football game. Tyler's right. You never see it, the guy lying on the field and then the medic giving him a shot."

"I'm concerned I made a mistake."

I said what everybody always said. "He's fine. Of course he's fine. He's Nate." Mr. Mullins called Nate a tough old bird, got the girls' gym teacher to watch us, and then escorted Nate down to the nurse's office. Everybody figured the nurse called his grandmother to take him to the hospital, forty minutes away.

When we went back to the classroom, Mrs. Anderson asked, "How is Mr. Emerling?" She meant Nate. She called us by our last names. We were supposed to write our first and last names on our papers, and then she assigned us all numbers that we always had to put next to our names.

I was number ten. I don't think she really knew our first names. It made it easier for the rest of us to forget them too.

Daniel answered first. "Unconscious."

"He is not," Homer said. "He'll be fine."

"He's getting a brain scan," Lucas announced.

Tyler said, "Homer knocked him out."

Mrs. Anderson turned to look around the room, because even if Homer was the new kid's real name she wouldn't know it. She was wondering who Homer was.

"It was an accident," Homer said.

"So I've heard," Mrs. Anderson told him. "The nurse called me. Sounds like quite a gym class for the first day of school."

Daniel said, "Homer could have saved him but he choked."

"Get your facts straight, Daniel," Lucas said. "Homer said he carries medicine for food allergies, not brain injuries. They're to save *him*, not a kid who can't duck." Lucas just kept doodling. He didn't even look at Daniel. But that's Lucas. If he's breathing, he has a pen or a pencil and he's drawing something.

"We were playing kickball," I started telling Mrs. Anderson, but I had to stop because I couldn't remember the new kid's real name. I wasn't going to call him Mister anything, and so the nickname came right out of my mouth. "And Homer," I said, "Homer threw the ball to get Nate out at first and it hit his head and knocked him out."

"Who?" Mrs. Anderson asked. I stuck my thumb at Homer. "Ah," she said, "Mr. Bishop."

"But he woke up," I said. "Nate."

Tyler said, "His head's not smashed or anything." Daniel mumbled something about how Homer could have saved Nate but didn't.

Nate didn't care. He was back the next day. He gave Homer a high five. "Homer! Now that's how to play kickball!"

Homer's grin was so big his cheeks were practically in his ears.

I wanted to tell him to stop looking so happy. Didn't he know? He was Homer forever. It didn't matter that he dropped the biggest kid in the sixth grade in his first gym class ever. It was like some kind of airport gift shop T-shirt: I WAS A GYM CLASS HERO AND ALL I GOT WAS THIS LOUSY NICKNAME.

CHAPTER 4

*A*FTER SCHOOL I rode my bike out to my job at the pheasant farm. I pedaled easy until I was out of sight of the school. Past the line of waiting buses (there's only four), past the row of houses all flying their Ohio State Buckeye flags, and past the football team my parents won't let me join. After that, everything is open. The land is flat and it rolls on and on. The sky stretches over the earth, edge to edge, everywhere you look. And then I go. Lung-bursting, leg-burning fast.

Out here is country. Nothing but sky and farms. There aren't a lot of trees—just a grouping every now and then by a house or in between fields. All the roads are straight and all the turns are right angles. Sometimes we get *Wizard of Oz* tornadoes like the one last week, but usually the most interesting weather is fog. Fog like cotton. So thick it's disorienting. When you look out the window in the morning, you might not be sure you're on the same planet you were on last night.

It was one of those hot and sunny days when you couldn't believe summer vacation was over and school had started. My bike helmet banged against my hip from where it hung off my backpack. I'd put it on once I was through the first stop sign and away from the school. I knew it was wrong to wait. In my mind I could hear my mom—my future sad mom—crying about it, saying how my brain was nothing but an unprotected watermelon.

It was also part of the deal for the job. Helmet on. Good grades.

Sometimes the road was all mine—all the space, all the pavement, all the sky, all the air—and I went as hard as I could and as fast as I could. Nothing else mattered. Not the itch. Not my tired legs. I only wanted to go. Maybe if I forgot everything I knew about everything, there could be lift-off, as if the Ohio wind could pick me up too, like a trampoline or a school roof caught in a storm, and give me a ride on the jet stream.

The yards and fields and trees I biked by were still littered with stuff. Pink insulation was caught in trees. At first, it had looked like a silly picture, like cotton candy decorations, but then it just looked like garbage.

I wasn't paying attention to the road and traffic, and then it was too late. A car came up fast behind me. It was going as fast as it could too. All growl like a beast. I knew

I didn't even have time to look over my shoulder, so I pointed my front wheel to the right and off the pavement. Me and bike, we hit the deep drainage ditch at the side of the road. It was the only escape. The car braked but never stopped and then sped away, screaming through the air.

Sometimes the ditches ran dry, but my luck wasn't that good. It was muddy and sludgy with farm runoff: dirt and chemicals and fertilizer, which usually means manure, which means you-know-what. It stank. I stank. It was cold too. I tried to remember if I had my lucky peanut shell with me. I thought I had it. So maybe my luck wasn't too bad. My bike and I were gross, but we were okay. It could have been worse.

When I got to the pheasant farm, Mr. Epple stood out in the yard.

"Hey," he said, "you stink." That's what he said. I didn't always understand him because sometimes he sounded like he had a mouthful of marbles, but I was sure about this. He was loud enough about it too.

"Yep."

I pulled my wet shirt away from my stomach. It fell right back again. Cold. Foul. I didn't say anything else. Mr. Epple didn't talk much and I didn't talk much and I think he liked it that way. What would I say, anyway? He was right. I stank.

I didn't always know what to make of Mr. Epple, but I liked the job. Riding on my bike. Getting paid. Taking it over from Sydney's brother Dylan so he could play football. Out here I wasn't Itch. Right then, though, with my shoes sludgy and my pants dark and wet, I felt like a freak, waiting to balloon with hives and swelling.

I didn't want the itch here. I didn't want it anywhere, but especially not here. But I was wet and cold and the odds were not in my favor.

Mr. Epple grunted at me. I think he said okay. Or go. He pointed to the pens.

"Right," I said, but he was already gone.

It was time for the dead check.

The pens where I worked were past Mr. Epple's house and a small red barn. It's called the brooder barn. Mr. Epple hatches eggs and raises pheasant chicks in the brooder barn until they're about six weeks old. Then they go to the pens.

The pens are made up of fat wood posts and chicken wire with something like chicken wire netting across the top. The birds don't have room to fly, even though the pen is called a flight pen. The birds scuttled around. They ran like chickens. Or took off low and landed again. Even though they're birds, they'd rather run than fly.

Inside the pens, it's a rectangle of a real bird world. Dirt and grass and plants and some bushes, and the birds.

The birds liked me. Well, they liked the food and water I had for them.

I've never seen one really fly. I bet it would be something. I've seen wild turkeys fly, big and heavy over the fields, and they're interesting because they don't look majestic or special or even birdlike. Not like a hawk, always on a mission. Once I saw a bald eagle by the river. It was huge, with shoulders like a football player. It was the biggest and most amazing animal I'd ever seen in the wild.

Pheasants are mean. Aggressive.

That's what Dylan had told me when he was training me for the job. Dylan is Sydney's middle brother. He's in ninth grade. He's the one who got me the job with Mr. Epple, right before his two-a-day practices for football started. "It's not much work," he'd said. "Mr. Epple doesn't talk much, but he's okay. Lets you just do your stuff. Wait till you see those birds fight! Bloodthirsty!"

The male ring-necked pheasants butt chests and fly at each other, their feet pointing at each other like weapons. They have spurs on their legs. They'll pluck out each other's feathers and then they'll bleed—and then all the roosters will want in. They'll peck each other to death. That's what Dylan told me.

The roosters called as I headed in. They sounded a little bit like a chicken rooster, but the call was short, like a cock-a-doodle-doo without the doodle-doo. It's squeaky and rusty sounding. The pen was all kicked-up dirt and crowing and the *drum-drum-drum* of wings flapping in a bird brawl.

Brutus was winning. The birds don't officially have names, but that's what I called the biggest, meanest bird in the first pen. He was the only bird Mr. Epple had to debeak. Every two weeks Mr. Epple grabbed Brutus and tucked him under his arm like a football and took a small knife to his bill, cut it precisely, and peeled back the top third of his beak. He still had a beak but it wasn't as sharp. It would grow back and Mr. Epple would snip it again. Mr. Epple said he might have to put Brutus in his own pen.

Brutus is also the name of the Ohio State mascot, which is a person in a costume with a scarlet-and-gray-striped sweater and a big nut head, but the name still sounds tough.

I ran into the pen, yelling and stomping, but the pheasants kept at it. I kicked at them even though I didn't know if that was allowed and scooped up the attacked bird. He'd been on his feet when I'd come in, screeching and flapping, but then he fell into my hands with his wings tucked in. The attacking birds didn't scatter right away and bobbed their heads, still wanting to peck.

The bird felt like a piece of grocery store chicken in my

hands, except it was long and feathered and it smelled. It didn't move. Its head was a dark and shimmering blue, like a puddle of gasoline, and a white ring went around its neck like a dog collar. Around each eye was a big red circular flap of skin. It looked lacy, like something in my grandma's house. Its feathers were broken or ruffled or plucked out, and blood oozed across its chest, and the fresh red blood blended in with its feathers. The body of a male pheasant is like the color of a mountain covered in fall leaves. Rust and yellow and brown.

With those colors it seemed like pheasants ought to be magnificent. I guess they are, since people pay to hunt them and stuff them and put them over their fireplaces, but I think they're goofy. Long legs. A long, outswept tail, like a broom or a rudder. They like to run from danger, not fly. They're like giant roadrunners playing dress-up.

"Go. Go on." I kicked at the pheasants still hanging out at my legs. They were probably just waiting for me to refill their food and water. Pecking birds to death: just another day at the office. "Get." They didn't.

Reaching into the orange bucket I carried for the dead check, I set the bird down gently. "Hey, bird," I said, "do you believe in luck?"

Except he's a bird with a bird brain so he never thought about anything much either way.

I pressed my lucky peanut shell to the white ring around his neck.

It didn't work. My lucky peanut shell. I knew that. I'm too smart for that. It's not like I could think otherwise, standing there in my wet and stinky clothes and holding a dead bird. Once, though, I believed it worked. For a while after I'd found the shell it was as though I'd figured out how to ignore the itch. It had seemed like magic. By the time I realized I still itched, carrying the peanut shell had become a habit. Habits are serious. Habits are burned into the animal part of your brain. So it doesn't always matter what the thinking part of your brain thinks because it might not always be in charge. So that was why I carried a good-luck charm that didn't work. Still, I was sorry. For the bird.

Mr. Epple was in the brooder barn, checking chicks and heat lamps. He was always checking chicks and heat lamps. If it was too cold, the chicks huddled up on each other and suffocated, and they'd die if it was too hot.

"Hey," I shouted, because I always needed to shout to get his attention. "Hey, Mr. Epple." I stepped into the barn with my bucket.

When Mr. Epple didn't answer I banged my fist against the rough wood of the barn. "I got a dead bird here."

Mr. Epple was tall and solid and I couldn't tell how old.

Grandfather old. But a tough old grandfather. He had short white hair that stuck up straight like a scrub brush and a flat face that my dad said meant he'd been punched a lot. My dad said he'd been a boxer.

"Mr. Epple?"

I waved my arms around, and when Mr. Epple finally came over I held up the bucket and showed him the bird.

"The others were pecking at him."

"What?"

"Bird fight. This guy lost." I might have told him more—there were three, they didn't want to stop, I kicked them away, I didn't know if that was allowed—but I knew extra words were useless. I wasn't always sure he was paying attention to me.

He nodded. "Yep." He took the bucket and poked at the bird. Giving the bucket back to me, he grabbed a shovel. "Follow me." He said it loud enough. I wondered if he thought I was stupid.

We took the bird out back to the fence line. A stretch of blue tarp was spread out on the ground and weighed down by rocks. Mr. Epple rolled the rocks away with his booted feet and then pulled the tarp back. There was a row of perfectly round holes, already dug, just waiting for dead birds. My mom had told me about stuff like this before I started working here. It was a farm job, she said. That meant the animals were not pets. "Just so you understand," she told me.

Mr. Epple pointed at the bucket and then one of the holes with his dirty hands. He handed me the shovel. "Cover it up." He made each word slowly and carefully. "Dirt, then tarp, and then rocks."

He headed back to the barn, and I followed my instructions. "Sorry I didn't get here sooner, bird." Guess I wasn't as bloodthirsty as Dylan. The sun was full yellow and hot, and shoveling in the dirt to cover the hole was hard work. My jeans hadn't dried yet. They stuck on me. At first, it kept me cool, my wet jeans and T-shirt, but then the more I moved and the hotter I got, the more they aggravated me. Like my clothes were going to get the itch started and do the itching for me. I didn't want the itch anywhere, but especially not here. No itching at the farm. It would be my third rule.

The second rule of itching is don't itch if there are witnesses. The first rule of itching is do not itch.

Yeah. Wish me luck with that.

CHAPTER 5

THE FOLLOWING DAY at lunch, the new kid sat next to me. "You're Itch," he said.

"That's me."

We were in the art room. The room stank like paint. Wet paintings hung on a clothesline in front of the chalkboard. There were a lot of drippy yellow and orange suns.

"Hi." Homer spread a paper towel over the paint-splattered table and arranged his lunch on top. Drink, sandwich, an apple, and a pack of chocolate chip cookies. Homer said, "You're the other allergic kid." He was smiling.

"Nope," I answered. Because we had no cafeteria and had to eat lunch in classrooms, we had to follow classroom rules, which meant no tree nuts, no peanuts, and no peanut butter. With peanut butter banned, I didn't know what to eat and had two slices of plain bread in a stack for my lunch. I ate them like a regular sandwich. "That's Sydney."

Sydney sat across from us. She lifted her sandwich and waved with it. "Yep," she said, "that's me."

"Oh," he said. "Hi."

I asked, "Do you want to move?" Because maybe he wanted to sit by Sydney.

His smile was gone. "Should I move?"

"You don't have to."

"Sorry. I thought you were the other kid with allergies. Why do they call you Itch, then?"

Nate, calling from the other end of the table, answered. "Because he itches. He itched so much one time he looked like a dead fish on the beach."

Homer looked me over.

Daniel piped up. "You ever see a dog just go crazy itching? He's got his tail thumping and he's whining and he's spinning himself in circles on the floor? That's Itch."

"Sheesh, come on, Daniel," Sydney said.

I didn't say anything. I didn't say anything about how when it had first happened I'd been sitting at my desk, not on the floor. I didn't say anything about the dog because if I could have itched like a dog, I would have. That's what it's like. That's the itch.

Homer turned and looked at me straight-on and apologized. He talked like he'd written it out ahead of time. "I'm sorry for thinking you were the other classmate with food allergies, and I apologize for the assumption I made about you. It's embarrassing."

Sydney said, "No worries," and so I said, "Yeah, sure."

"Good. Great." He started eating his lunch. "What are you allergic to, Sydney?"

Sydney said, "Dairy and peanuts. Sesame seeds. You know, EpiPens in the nurse's office."

"Oh," Homer said, pointing to a big lump in his pocket. "I carry mine."

Sydney tossed her braid over her shoulder. "Yeah, I heard all about it. I can't believe the guys thought Nate needed it."

Homer said, "They were trying to help." He turned to me and asked, "What are you allergic to?"

I told him I wasn't allergic to anything.

"He's allergic to *jeans*," Nate said.

Homer looked at my legs. I was wearing jeans.

Nate wasn't done. "He's allergic to *school*. He's allergic to the *air*. He's allergic to *nothing*."

That's when I got it, how summer friends and summer rules and school friends and school rules are different. Nate wouldn't have said that when we were hanging out on our bikes with Sydney, but when we fell into place for the sixth grade, we didn't fall into the same places we were in the summer.

Daniel said, "Itch is allergic to spelling tests," which was amazing because Daniel never remembers anything. He's the guy who likes to smack his forehead to show off just how much he can forget, but he remembered this. He was right too. The first big itch had happened during a spelling test. I still remember the words. *Vacant, cavern, punish, legal, fatigue.* I don't even *like* those words. I get itchy just *seeing* those words.

"I am not," I said. "I'm not allergic to tests."

"Oh," Homer said, and then he went through the list of what he was allergic to again. "I'm allergic to dairy, peanuts, and tree nuts. I'm allergic to pretty much all the nuts people eat. But not acorns. Not that I want to eat acorns, but I guess I could. If I wanted. I don't. I mean, who does?"

Nate said, "I've eaten acorns." Everybody laughed, but he was probably telling the truth.

Homer looked concerned. "I hope they weren't raw."

Nate shrugged.

Homer said, "When I was a one-year-old, all I could eat was coconut milk, rice, mangoes, and avocadoes. Avocadoes are very nutritious, if you didn't know."

Daniel asked, "What's avocado?"

Tyler said, "It's green. It's guacamole."

Daniel pretended to gag.

Sydney said, "My mom would have a heart attack."

Homer shrugged. "It's okay. I'm a good egg."

"It sounds like it really stinks," I said.

The new kid took a sip of something that wasn't milk and said, "My mom says, Get better, not bitter."

"Hear that, Itch? All you got to do is get all better. Cured."

Homer's eyes turned sharp on Nate and he said, "That's not what it means at all." He turned to me. "What are they talking about?"

I took a bite of my air sandwich. Two pieces of soft bread. I chewed and chewed so I didn't have to talk.

It wasn't like I could explain it to Homer. It was hard enough for me to understand.

Here's how the itch happens: no one knows how it happens. The word for it is *idiopathic*, which means it just happens, it's just me, there is no specific known cause to explain it.

It shows up out of nowhere. Or if I'm cold. Or if I'm warm and the room is cold. Or maybe just because I'm pressing my arms on my desk during a test. Or if I think about itching. Maybe the itch starts with my pinky finger. It might feel colder than my other fingers, and then, bam, it's filled with heat and itch. Even if I don't itch, it feels like my skin is too tight. One size too small. Like my bones are growing but not my skin.

Sometimes it's a spot on my foot that itches.

Or a red spot at the base of my thumb.

If I touch that red spot, it's like a switch that turns everything on and sends out a signal—a hot, electric web of itches all throughout my body, running over my skin and getting as deep into me as it can. I give up and I give in, let it ride through me like a supernatural being, and itch and itch and itch until that beast is loose.

Itching it makes it all worse. The first time it happened, though, I didn't even know to *think* about not itching. I felt an itch so I did what any one would do and scratched. Fingernail to the palm of my hand. Maybe I should have known something was up, because isn't that a strange place to get an itch? But I didn't even think about it. I itched. And then I itched and I itched and I itched.

Everywhere I itched turned swollen. It started as puffiness, and then my hands were fat, my knuckles gone. I couldn't even make a fist. I still managed to itch, though, and rubbed my hands on my legs, rolled my toes in my shoes, pressed one foot on top of the other until it hurt. Streaks of itch flamed across my cheeks, and by then I had my shoulders up, trying to press them against my face. The itch ran down my arms, my back, my legs. Everywhere. I could feel it spreading, growing, every time I touched my skin, anytime anything touched my skin.

The teacher came over and I must have looked hideous because she whispered, which is unusual for a teacher. Or maybe she didn't whisper. My ears itched too, and maybe I was swollen there and maybe I couldn't hear.

The school nurse called my mom, who took me to the emergency room. At the ER I got antihistamines.

I hadn't swelled up on the inside. My breathing was good. My heart rate and blood pressure were fine. In four hours, it was all over and I'd learned my lesson. Do not itch. Under any circumstances. Even if it's impossible. Even if it's the hardest work of my life. Even if I can't do it—even if I can't *not itch*. Itching is not the answer. It is never the answer. It was the most important thing I'd learned from all of the fifth grade.

Remember the first rule of itching? Do not itch.

Itching doesn't solve anything. Itching an itch doesn't make it stop itching. It's a trick, and I fall for it every time. It doesn't matter that I know better. It doesn't matter that I have a lucky peanut shell. My dad says that's insanity. He says insanity is doing the same thing over and over again and thinking you'll get different results. That doing the same thing will make something else happen that didn't happen the last time. Itching always does the same thing to me. It makes my skin go hot and streak with red and swell, first in hives and then in welts that grow together until I'm puffy and swollen and nothing but nostrils.

"The only thing that matters," Nate said to Homer, "is if you're allergic to the Buckeyes."

"Not the nut," Sydney said. "The Ohio State University Buckeyes."

"Yeah," said Tyler, "because if you're allergic to the Buckeyes you can't sit here." Tyler wore a sport T-shirt or jersey every day. Today he wore a Cleveland Cavaliers shirt.

"That's the only thing," Nate repeated.

Homer said what everybody in Ohio always says. "I bleed scarlet and gray."

From across the room, Abby called out, "Go Bucks!"

Homer's grin still hung on his face. "You guys know the Buckeye Bus? That's ours. Well, my dad's. My dad's and my uncles'. We share. Most of the time."

"No way!"

"I've seen it!"

"That's you?"

"I can't believe it!"

Everybody knows the Buckeye Bus. It drives around town on Thursdays and Fridays, and on Sundays after a win. It's not around on Saturdays. On Saturdays it's in Columbus at the football stadium, the Horseshoe, or somewhere near there, tailgating. It's an old gray school bus decked out in Ohio State colors with a scarlet stripe down its middle to look like a Buckeye football helmet. Sure, there are plenty of special red-and-silver cars driving around with special stickers and flags and all sorts of stuff, but around here the Buckeye Bus is the biggest and best of them.

"Have you ever taken it Up North?"

Up North is our archrival. When you're talking football, you don't ever say the name of that school or its state. It's north of Ohio. We share a border. It's the one everybody likes to say is shaped like a mitten.

"My father has. One time, after OSU won, the Buckeye Bus broke down. No one stopped to help. He said not even the state trooper that drove by, but I think he was exaggerating."

Sydney said, "I've seen it around town. It's really cool."

Homer nodded and told her, "Thank you. The bus has had more mechanical problems than we can fix. This might be our last season. So, you know, we've got to be National Champs."

Daniel and Tyler fist-bumped. "National Champs, baby!"

Nate took a bite of cold chicken nugget and said what I'd been waiting for him to say. "The only person who's allergic to the Buckeyes around here is Itch."

CHAPTER 6

DAD WAS WAITING for me on the porch when I got home from school that afternoon, so I was glad I hadn't taken my helmet off early like I do sometimes. "Hey there," he said, smiling through the scruff of the new beard he was growing.

"Hey." Now that I'd stopped riding the bike—my own personal wind machine—the sweat caught up with me. Dad met me on the front step and, reaching down, grabbed the handlebars and hauled my bike the rest of the way up.

"Do you have homework?"

"Not much."

Looking at his watch, he said, "You've got time to clean up before the barbecue at Sydney's tonight. And then homework and talk to your mom."

"Did Mrs. Warren say if there'll be brats?"

That made Dad grin. "She didn't, as a matter of fact, but I've never known them to serve anything else at a barbecue."

"I won't tell Mom if you don't tell Mom. She hates brats. She says they're unhealthy."

Dad held his hands up and said, "I'm not keeping any secrets from her. Besides, as soon as we tell her about the barbecue she'll know what we ate."

"True."

"She wants to video chat soon."

"It's so slow. Email works for me."

Dad scratched his unshaven chin. Like a baseball player in the play-offs, he wasn't going to shave until the job was over and Mom came back. Watching him scratch made me itchy, and Dad was doing it all the time now, scratching his chin. "She wants to see you. Moms and dads are funny like that."

We walked over to the barbecue. Like everybody else in Ohio, Sydney's family is serious about their Buckeyes. They have an Ohio State flag and also a stone goose at the front door that they dress up in Buckeye gear. By their front steps they have a flat garden stepping-stone with the Ohio State logo on it, and I've never seen one drop of bird poop on it because someone actually keeps the thing clean.

Everybody speaks Buckeye like it's its own language, and I'm just not a natural. I'm getting the hang of it. I'm better than I used to be. And now there was a Homer. The new kid. He might bleed scarlet and gray, but *I'd* spent the summer hanging out with Nate and Daniel and Tyler and Sydney. Everybody but Sydney called me Itch, but it was just a name. Over the summer, it didn't mean anything.

I usually watch the games with Sydney at her house. It's always a party. I usually start out watching the game by myself in my living room, and then Sydney shows up, climbing through the bushes at the front of house and sticking her face right up against the window next to the television and knocking. At her house, there are snacks and cheering people who rise up out of their seats for the big hits. We eat brats. Brats—bratwurst—are sausage-y hot dogs but bigger, and people boil them in beer and then grill them. They're the best thing about Ohio. Probably a lot of people outside Ohio eat brats but I never had any until we moved here and we started hanging out at Sydney's. We ate brats on football Saturdays and when we worked together on our math homework.

When I study at Sydney's house, the dining room table is crowded with her and her two older brothers, me, and everybody's books and notebooks, and then her dad always comes in and drops off a big platter of brats and a pile of paper plates. Everybody talks with their mouth full. The table is too crowded for her parents, so no one tells us to finish chewing before we start talking. My parents would never let me study that way, with distractions. They'd never let me eat that way either.

Last year, in the fifth grade, we started multiplying fractions and dividing fractions in simple cases. How many one-third-cup servings are in two cups of raisins? How much rice do nine people get if they divide up a fifty-pound bag equally?

"The answer," I said to Sydney as we tried to keep the ketchup and mustard off our homework, "is too much. It's too many raisins for everybody. It's too much rice."

Dylan said, "Maybe they're making rice pudding."

"You can make pudding out of rice?"

"Sure," Sydney said.

"Is it good?" I couldn't imagine that it would be good.

"It's okay," she said at the same time her oldest brother, Evan, said, "No." He sat at the head of the table. He was in the tenth grade then. He was as big as a grown-up. He was the backup quarterback on the high school football team.

Sydney said, "It's not my favorite. Rice pudding. But it's dessert."

"Anyway," Dylan said, "it doesn't matter. Only the numbers matter in a math problem."

"You always do this," Sydney said to me. "You try to argue about the problem instead of just getting it done."

"I do not."

"Just follow the steps."

"Aren't your parents engineering geniuses?" That was Dylan.

"What? They just have jobs. Those are just their jobs."

"*Math* jobs. How were you not born not doing fractions and long division in your head?"

I shrugged. Sydney told her brother to butt out. Her mom came in and switched the empty brat platter with a plate of homemade sunflower seed butter buckeye candies. That's another thing that's big here in Ohio. Buckeye candies. Usually they're balls of peanut butter dipped in chocolate. But since Sydney is allergic to peanut butter, her mom makes them with SunButter. Those are good too. The real buckeye, which is a nut, is inedible unless you boil it for hours or something, and even then no one wants to eat it. Except maybe Nate.

"Thanks, Mrs. Warren," I said. And then because it was true, I said, "Brats and buckeyes are pretty much my favorite thing about Ohio."

She said I was welcome and then I said, "Because I was really worried that first weekend here when we ordered the pizza."

Dylan wanted to know what was wrong with the pizza.

Sydney flung herself back in her chair and moaned, "Not this again!"

"It's rectangular. That's what's wrong with the pizza."

Dylan stared at me. But it was true. He couldn't argue with me. The pizza here is rectangular. It's one of the worst things about Ohio. When people get together to cheer on the Buckeyes, they eat rectangular pizza. It gets me every time. Rectangular pizza. And then it's cut into even smaller rectangles or squares. Not triangles. It's like making a square apple pie or something. And everybody knows the crust is the best part. When pizza is cut into triangles, every piece has crust. If you get pizza cut into squares you're going to run out of the good stuff fast. It doesn't help that this town is so small the only place to eat out just happens to be the gas station that also makes its own sheets of pizza. It's not very good.

Dad and I were right about the brats. We could smell them cooking all through the neighborhood. "Yes!" Dad and I high-fived. I loved a party at Sydney's. I was going to get to eat brats and chips, and the only vegetable was going to be the ketchup.

We'd never had a back-to-school barbecue before, and I'm pretty sure the only reason we were having one this year, to start the sixth grade, was because Sydney's mom was worried about me and my dad because my mom was in China. I knew it for sure when it turned out Dad and I were the only guests. Even Sydney's brothers weren't there because they both had football practice. This year, Evan was the starting quarterback.

"You two can't live on food from the Chinese place," Sydney's mom said to us as we went to the back deck.

I told Mrs. Warren, "We don't get Chinese much," and I was pretty sure she knew that the only thing stopping us from eating it every night was that the closest Chinese restaurant is nearly an hour away, in the same town with the hospital. First it's long country roads with tractors, threshers, and harvesters rattling alongside you in the fields, ghosting up seeds and dirt and fibers. Then, before the town, come the factories and plants. The foundry that makes car engines. It's a huge building surrounded by parking lots and gates and railroad tracks, and it smells. There's the plant where both my parents work. Then the place that makes soup. I'd heard some people say that Nate's dad used to work there until he was fired for swimming in a tank of soup water. After the factories comes the town's strip—car dealers and banks and gas stations and a grocery store and a couple of fast-food places and the Chinese place, which is between the dollar store and a fish aquarium place.

Sydney told me she never eats Chinese food. She's worried about the peanuts and the oils and the sesame seeds in the teriyaki and all the other dishes she can't see them in. Once I asked her if she couldn't just pick them off, the sesame seeds, and she told me no way.

Mr. Warren turned his grilling fork on me. It was like a small pitchfork. "Kid! What are you wearing? Are you a Boilermaker or something?"

"What?" I didn't know what Mr. Warren was talking about.

"It's your shirt," Sydney told me. "It's yellow. And your ball cap is black."

That didn't really clear things up for me.

"A boilermaker is an ironworker," Dad said.

Sydney, sprawled out on a cushy patio chair, sat up fast and looked at me as if it were an emergency. "My dad means you like Purdue. Purdue University. Their colors are yellow and black."

"Don't worry, son," Sydney's dad said, his barbecue fork still aimed at me, "we'll make a Buckeye out of you yet." Turning to my dad, he asked, "So who do you like for the starting quarterback?"

My dad laughed a little. "I have enough trouble remembering not to mow the lawn on a Saturday afternoon, let alone keep track of all the quarterbacks."

Sydney's dad started to laugh. Really laugh, as though what my dad said was really, really funny. He didn't know my dad was being totally straight with him. And my dad didn't know that all the Buckeye sports news was about the three quarterbacks sitting on the football coach's bench.

So you can see that what Nate had said about me being allergic to Buckeye football wasn't really that far off.

Instead of watching the game, my parents go grocery shopping. Unless my dad's been called in to work, which happens sometimes on Saturdays when the computers and machines need to be reset. Then Mom is disappointed because I never want to go with her. She says it's the best time to go because the stores are empty. Do you know where I watched last year's big OSU–That Team Up North game? At the empty food court in the mall, sixty miles away.

Even though it was game day and we were all at the mall, we were out of place. Everybody else there was dressed in their full Buckeye gear, as if it were dangerous to go out without it. Jerseys. Sweatshirts. Ball caps. Not us. We were like aliens who had dropped down from another state or another planet.

That was last November. Before everybody started calling me Itch, before the tornado ate our cafeteria, and before my mom got on an airplane for China.

Now, at the barbecue, I loaded my brat up with ketchup and mustard, and Mrs. Warren asked me how I liked the job at the pheasant farm.

"Dylan was sorry to give it up," she said, "but football takes all his extra time now."

Dad said, "It's Isaac's as long as he keeps his grades up."

"Study session at the Warren house," Sydney said.

We bumped fists. Sydney made a soft explosion noise as our hands came away from each other. "Sixth-grade fractions, here we come." Then she asked, "How long is your mom going to be gone again?"

"A long time," I told her. "Until November, right, Dad?"

Dad said, "That's the plan. But you know your mom. She might be done ahead of schedule. Fingers crossed." He rubbed his chin.

Sydney looked at me and whispered, "Your dad's beard is going to be crazy. Do you think your mom will even recognize him when she comes home?"

"Who knows?" I answered, my mouth full.

"He's starting to look a little scary." She still whispered. "And it's only been, what? A week? Do you think he'll grow his hair long too? By the time the World Series rolls around, those guys look like Bigfoot."

We both started laughing and I nearly choked and I spit out some of my food.

Sydney said, "I wouldn't be able to stand it if my mom was away. Just me and my dad and brothers. I mean, as much as I like them, it would be all brats all the time."

"You should be so lucky. Mom doesn't let us eat them at home. She says they're unhealthy."

"Your mom thinks football is unhealthy."

"True." I took a big bite of my brat. My eyes were still watering and I was still coughing from laughing before.

Sydney asked, "Do you miss her?"

I guzzled my drink and nodded and coughed some more until my nose burned from the root beer.

CHAPTER 7

WHEN WE GOT home from the barbecue at Sydney's I said good night to Dad and went down the creaky stairs to the basement.

Then I stuck my head back into the stairwell to call to Dad. "Hey, what's this?"

He asked, "What's what?" but he knew.

"You moved my Buckeye poster down here." It was a birthday present from Sydney last year. The Ohio State University football team taking the field in their scarlet uniforms and their silver helmets with the marching band behind them, the gold tubas pointing up to the sun. Brutus, the mascot, ran in front, carrying the school flag.

"The room looked a little bare," he said.

"How about we get a foosball table? And a pool table? Maybe a home theater? To watch the games?"

Dad laughed.

"Its edges are curling up. The poster's."

He tossed me a roll of masking tape and told me I had a perfectly fine room upstairs. "It's lonely up here."

"I'll be back."

"Good," he said. "When?"

"Sometime." I made loops of tape and fixed the poster, and Dad called down again to tell me to email Mom.

Her email was a long list of questions. There were typos. She never makes typos. She's a detail person. Once, she returned a loaf of bread to a bakery because it had too many air bubbles in it. Dad shouted, "It's an act of God!" but Mom said, no, it was shoddy workmanship.

I tried to picture her at work, in a factory, on the other side of the world, or in her hotel room, writing me an email, and I knew she was tired. Because she never makes mistakes. She fixes mistakes. And I kind of wanted to tell her not to write, not if she was so tired the mistakes made it look like someone else wrote the message.

She wanted to know if I was warm enough, if I'd gotten any hives, about the weather, about school, what my friends were up to, what it was like without a cafeteria, if Dad was feeding me enough, what I ate for lunch since I could no longer bring a peanut butter sandwich, if I wore my bike helmet.

China is an even twelve hours ahead, so it was easy to

keep track of the time difference. It was seven at night here and so it was morning there. She called sometimes. The connection wasn't very good. It cut in and out and we kept losing sentences.

I wrote, *Dad says you might be home ahead of schedule.*

She wrote back right away. *He's an optimist. Does your lucky peanut shell still work?*

Not for pheasants, I wrote.

Her next answer was all typos. *Dsn't mean it's stilll not lucky..for you.*

She thinks like that. She thinks all the small stuff is big stuff. When the cafeteria roof was spread out in pieces for miles in the fields it only made the local weekly newspaper. We didn't even make the television news station, an hour away. All those weather folks who talked through the Buckeye game didn't care. Mom told me that something didn't have to make the news to be important. If it was important to me then it was important.

I'd found the peanut shell in our yard last spring doing yard work, raking up any soggy, leftover leaves we'd missed that fall. It was open and empty and cleaned by the weather. Some of it was missing. It felt papery.

When I found it, I felt the itch and it was the first time I didn't give in and scratch. I thought I could control it.

Because I could, then, that day, and for a while after. Then. I believed that. I thought it might be magic. I didn't know it was just a coincidence. I didn't know keeping a good-luck charm might just be a habit.

I kept it with me since then, the shell. But it was kind of hard to keep. I had to keep it a secret. It was embarrassing. I didn't need anyone at school finding out about it. And it was crumbly. It ended up snapped nearly in half. Just a few fibers held it together. I usually stuck it into my pocket. I didn't always remember to take it out again before I put my clothes in the laundry, though Mom or Dad always found it and gave it back to me. Right before she left for China, Mom gave me a special box for it, a small black jewelry-store box.

I reread Mom's sloppy note and typed, *Eat your breakfast Mom. It's the most important meal of the day.*

I wondered what her hotel was like. Was it like ones we stayed in on our trips back to New York to visit my grandparents? Did it have a pool she wouldn't use and plates of cookies at the front desk and a breakfast bar with a waffle maker?

Mom's answer flashed at me. *Eat your breakfast, Mom. Comma!*

I sent her a smiley face.

Mom: *Aw, that warms my heart. Looks just like you (ha ha ha). How's school?*

Me: *It's only the first week. Nothing to report. The teacher likes to call us by our last names.*

I didn't tell her that everybody but Sydney was still calling me Itch, same as last year, or that how I itched was a big topic of conversation, or that explaining everything about me to the new kid was so entertaining for all the guys, it erased most of the fun we'd had over the summer.

Then she went back to luck and sent this: *Wanted to tell you about a study I read that said people who believe in luck think they have better luck. What do you think?*

Me: *Sounds unscientific.*

Mom: *No harm in trying it.*

CHAPTER 8

*I*F I'M FAST getting out of school, I can get my bike unlocked and get on the road before the buses pull out. It's a race. If I lose, the assistant principal and Mr. Mullins hold the leftover kids back until the yellow buses chug out of the parking lot. Today I lost, but only because I was talking with Sydney about Halloween costumes and then we walked out toward her bus together.

"The best homemade costume I ever saw was a girl as a gumball machine," I said. "She had on tights and stuff and had all these different colored balloons all over her."

"Nah. I want to be original, Isaac. I think I should do scary this year."

"It was a long time ago," I said. "It was back in New York. It's not a repeat for here."

"I'll think about it. I don't know why I'm thinking about it. I just don't want to be a cookie again. My mom is really into me being a cookie. Like, as an encore."

"You were a good cookie." She was chocolate chip. She

wore two circles of yellow poster board—one on the front and one on the back—with big brown circles on them.

"Too babyish for sixth grade."

"Well, yeah, but you wore it in the *fifth* grade."

That made her laugh and that made me laugh. I was on a roll. "Maybe you just need to step it up. Be a zombie cookie."

We stood laughing in front of her bus.

"You should come by later. After my dance class. We can do our math together. This is the year of fractions. *Fraaaac-tions.* Uncommon *de-noooom-inators.*" She said it in a vampire voice. "I know all about it from my brothers."

"So far it's just review from last year," I said. "I got it."

"Okay. If you're sure. I'll come get you to watch the game on Saturday. I've got dance class first, so I won't be home until halftime. But I'll watch the rest. Second Big Ten game of the season. Iowa."

"We'll beat them, no problem."

"You know it."

After that, I had to wait for all the buses to leave. The football team, loaded up with pads and helmets, had already jogged out for practice. They lay in the field, stretching. I didn't know Evan's and Dylan's numbers. I couldn't tell who was who.

Standing on the pedals, I rode my bike slowly through

the grass and by the chain link fence around the athletic field. Nate, Daniel, and Tyler, hung up on the fence like bats (but not upside down), watching.

"Hope they're meditating, lying there," Daniel said. "Hope they're working on their mental game. They're going to need it this Friday, playing those giants." You might think Daniel was offering good advice, but he's got a mean streak. He wasn't really trying to come up with a way to help the football team out. He was saying they were puny chickens.

Tyler said, "All the teams are bigger than us."

"We've got farm boys," Nate said. "Farm boys are big."

Daniel said, "That's old-school. All those other teams? They have fancy weight rooms."

We were quiet for a while. The players on the field scrambled up like a bunch of awkward, high-school-sized Frankensteins.

"Hey," Tyler said, "I saw you talking with Sydney."

"Yeah." Sydney and I have been friends since I moved here. It doesn't matter that she's a girl. It's been like that since the third grade. It isn't any kind of boy-girl thing. We watched football and rode our bikes together and played cards and we cooked dairy-free and peanut-free desserts in her kitchen. Giant oatmeal cookies and choc-olate chip pumpkin bread, but I wasn't going to tell these guys that. Plus, they'd want to eat it all. "Halloween costume discussion."

"So important," Tyler said.

"Very important," Daniel said.

Last year we all went together. We did all the streets here and then Tyler's dad drove us to one of the rich neighborhoods in the next town. Everybody goes to that neighborhood. I guess it's a big deal and not everybody who lives there likes it—giving out hundreds of mini chocolate bars—and one lady said she didn't think we lived around there because she could smell the farm on our shoes.

It was Tyler. It was always Tyler. It was Tyler's pig farm shoes, which always smelled even though they never looked dirty. Or his jacket. The lady still dropped a single candy bar into each of our bags. Tyler said, "Thank you," but Daniel said, "I hope you enjoy your bacon," and right then I liked his mean streak. Right then it wasn't a mean streak, it was just backbone and he was using his power for good. When we got farther down the street, Tyler said what he said at school. "What's that smell? Oh, that smell? It's money-money-money-money."

Out on the field, the coaches blew whistles and the players ran drills. Tyler dropped down from the fence first and yelled, "Tire swing!"

"Yes!"

They started running toward the playground. "You coming?" Tyler asked.

"Working," I said.

Nate pointed at Daniel. "You're pushing." They were going to play the game where one person sat in the tire swing and the guys whipped it in circles with all their strength until the one in the swing begged for mercy or some teacher finally came out of the building and said what we were doing wasn't a very good idea.

As they headed back toward the empty playground, Nate hollered, "Itch! You coming by later?"

"Sure," I hollered back, pushing my bike through the grass to the road.

I spotted the circling turkey vultures before I even got close to Mr. Epple's farm. The birds were big, hulking, and ugly, with red and wrinkled featherless heads. Coasting, they cruised for dead meat. The dead meat would be dead pheasants, the way the turkey vultures skimmed low over the pens. They wouldn't get any, though. They wouldn't get any pheasants. They couldn't get into the pens. I knew that. But I also knew there were dead birds inside the pen and that it wouldn't be like last time with only one sad bird pecked to death.

I was right. I found three dead birds without heads. Three birds was a lot. The headless bodies lay around the edges of the pen, against the fence. One was a female. The hens aren't as big as the males and they aren't as colorful— just a kind of not-white with brown patterns on their feathers. If it weren't for the male, everybody would think that the hens were pretty too.

I didn't find their heads until later. For the males, they were all torn off right at the white ring around the male neck, as if it meant *Open Here.*

Had the birds done this to each other? In a massive bird brawl? I wondered about that until I found Brutus. I knew it was him because of his clipped beak. No pheasant rooster in the pen would rip off Brutus's head, even if Brutus was debeaked. As far as I knew, pheasants didn't rip off heads, anyway.

It must have been something, whatever came after Brutus. I didn't know what. The fencing was buried deep to stop critters from digging their way in.

I went looking for Mr. Epple. He wasn't anywhere. Not in the yard where I'd seen him before. There was nothing inside the brooder barn but warming lamps and chicks. I marked down the three birds from the dead check in the grubby notebook that hung by a string nailed in the wall next to the door. I knocked on the house's back door. *Knock knock knock.* When he didn't answer: *pound pound pound.*

A big delivery truck rumbled as it turned into the long

driveway, and I finally saw Mr. Epple at the mailbox. He stood at the edge of the road with his back to the truck, setting up a piece of plywood that folks on country roads use to keep the snowplows from knocking down their mailboxes. It seemed early for it, since it was only September, but you never knew about the weather. Even though he was practically standing in the road, I swear Mr. Epple never looked at the truck, never saw it, and the truck never stopped.

"Hey! Hey! Stop! Mr. Epple!"

I ran harder than I ever had in gym class, but trucks are fast and kids are slow. I was slow. I wasn't fast enough. The truck turned hard. Mr. Epple didn't look up and kept hammering the plywood to the post of his mailbox. He didn't notice anything. Not me running and shouting and not the big truck aimed at him.

I thought of me diving with my bike into the ditch to dodge the car. I thought about how the car didn't come out of nowhere, not really, how I heard that screaming air, the buzz of engine, how my skin started to crawl a second before the real danger was there in the form of a big one-ton machine that could grind me up and turn me into watermelon pulp.

When Mr. Epple finally looked up I was ready to tackle him like a Buckeye lineman with a silver-bullet helmet. I just ran and ran and knew what I had to do. If he wouldn't move, I would move him. I ran right into him. He banged up off the road, against the mailbox and the plywood, and as I skidded, the mailbox got me in the gut. "Sorry, sorry." Finally he saw the truck and the driver saw us and the brakes hissed.

Mr. Epple opened his mouth but said nothing. I knew, though. I knew he was working hard on something to say that he didn't want to give up. I waited and waited and waited.

The delivery truck driver threw open his door and yelled, "Sorry," even though his face said, *Stupid people.* "Everybody okay?"

Mr. Epple's mouth was still open. He looked at the driver but didn't speak, so I held up a hand. It was supposed to mean we were fine. Guess I didn't feel like talking either.

That's when I figured it out. It hit me like that truck had just kept going. Boom. Mr. Epple couldn't hear.

After the truck driver dropped off a couple of boxes and left, Mr. Epple gave my shoulder a solid thump and nodded and didn't say anything, so I didn't say anything. We walked out to the fence line to bury the birds. I wanted to know what happened to them but didn't ask.

Nate's grandmother's storage units were between the farm and my house. That's where Nate hung out. He played one-man dodgeball in whatever empty unit his grandmother would let him. It wasn't always the same one, but it was always easy to find him. I just listened for banging metal.

It was dark inside and the game was loud. The ball ricocheted off the half-open metal door and rebounded on the concrete and blasted off the walls. We didn't say anything, just played until we were panting. It was wild.

After a while, we stopped to catch our breath. "Anybody get sick on the tire swing?"

"Nah," Nate said. "How are the birds?"

I told him about the dead pheasants. He thought it was cool. I couldn't find the words to say anything about the rest of what happened.

Bang. The ball shot off the metal door. "Owl," Nate said. "Got to be an owl, right?" He swooped out one arm in slo-mo and turned his hand into a claw and made like he was grabbing a pheasant. "If one of the birds is sitting up high—are there bushes and stuff in the pens?"

I nodded.

"So," Nate continued, "he can't get it through the fence.

The owl. And the pheasant can't get out. Pop." He turned his claw back into a hand and I could imagine just what had happened. Except for maybe why the owl dropped the heads.

Nate said, "If a mink or weasel got in, they just kind of nibble on the back of the head and leave the bodies. You'd have found a stack of three birds with holes in their heads."

"Right." Of course Nate knew this stuff.

When he told me he had a chart about different animals and how they killed, I laughed and I forgot about knocking Mr. Epple over.

"Skunks," he announced, grinning, "just eat the *entrails* and leave everything else. I've never seen a skunk kill. Promise you'll call me if a skunk gets into those pens."

"Won't happen. I mean, I'd call you, but a skunk will never get in. Epple's got fencing, like, buried three feet down and out."

"That owl. Three times. What's that about? Stupid bird." Nate dribbled the ball and changed his mind. "Maybe it was a smart bird."

"Wouldn't the heads still be in the owl's claws? Wouldn't he want those?"

Nate shrugged.

I figured it out. "When the owl catches the pheasant its claws are inside the pen. The owl has to let go to get his feet back."

We slapped the ball around for a while. Then Nate said, "I want a chick. My grandma said she'll give me one of the units. I was thinking chickens, but pheasants would be cool."

"You'd need heat lamps. A storage unit would be too cold for chicks."

"It'll toughen them up."

"Yeah, toughen them up until they're dead."

"Maybe you could get me a hen. You know, to sit on them."

"I don't think Mr. Epple sells the birds, except to the preserves. You can order pheasants from some stores. They sell them at Tractor Supply."

"I know they do. But you can get me one for free, right? We're friends."

"Come on, Nate." I started to wish I hadn't stopped by. I didn't want to be part of one of his bad ideas. The only thing was you usually didn't know the good ideas from the bad ones until you were in the middle of them. Aside from Sydney, I spent the most time with Nate. Sydney and I used to hang out, easy, after school, before school, all summer, but I got busy with the farm and her mom drives her to ballet lessons twice a week, an hour away, and then on the other days she's got soccer. She hung out more with Abby and Maria now. One thing was for sure: Sydney would never ask me to steal her a pheasant.

"I'll come around and you can give me a bird and you just tell the farmer that the bird died or whatever you do."

"That's stealing."

"That old farmer would never miss it." Nate looked at me for a long time. I was stuck. I didn't know what to say. I'd already said no. But then Nate said, "Never mind," and dribbled the ball a couple of times and then hooked it under his arm. We stood like that for a couple of minutes, and then I left.

I headed by Sydney's but her dad told me she wasn't home. He and Dylan and Evan were unloading the boys' practice gear from the car. "She's still at soccer," Dylan said. His hair was sweaty and it stuck out all over the place.

I said bye and looked up at the oak tree that had caught Sydney's bike, because I always had to look, and biked home under the power lines that were back up on the poles where they belonged.

Dad wasn't home yet. I went downstairs. In the quiet of the basement I remembered what it had been like when the power had been out for five days. Weird. No background noise. No fridge running, no air conditioner, no computer humming. Peaceful. Eerie.

Pressing my hands hard over my ears, I listened. The house still whirred. I still heard the blood in my brain, or in my hands, or somewhere on the inside.

After a while, I turned on my computer.

Hey, Mom,
What are you doing?
Have you looked at the stars yet?
Have you seen the moon?
Did you know that Mr. Epple can't really hear anything?
Do you think I should get Nate a bird?
Get means steal.
Why do my friends call me the thing I hate about myself?
If I really sent this to you, what would you say?

Then I pressed down on the backspace key until it ate up all the words.

CHAPTER 9

*I*TCH, HEY, WAIT up!" Nate huffed up behind me. It was morning. Cold and not quite foggy. Milky, the weather guy on TV called it. I walked my bike over to the rack in front of school and Nate followed me. "I'm serious about a bird," he said, putting both hands on the rack's top bar as he leaned over to watch me lock up my bike. "I'm thinking, though, I should get two birds. Makes more sense. Two birds."

"Two birds?"

"You mad at me?"

"Not really." It was too stupid to be mad about, right? And why did he want a bird so much? Why did he want a bird from *me*?

"Nah," he said, "you're mad. I know mad."

It didn't matter if I was and if Nate knew it, because he hadn't changed his mind. He still wanted to convince me to do it. "Look, you told me about the dead check. Just tell the old guy a couple of birds died and you already incinerated them—"

"What? I don't burn them."

"Oh." He pulled on the straps of his backpack. "Well, what do you do?"

"I bury them." I clunked my bike lock shut.

"Okay, so you tell the old guy you buried them and I'll just come by to the fence and get them."

I didn't say that Mr. Epple wasn't really that old, or that I wasn't going to steal.

Instead I said, "It's not a very good plan. I mean, I'm going to have two live birds and they aren't going to want to get carried around like fancy puppies. And how am I supposed to get them through the fence?"

"They're birds. They'll fly. And then I'll get them."

"Seriously? I know you're a hunter and everything, but do you think it'll be that easy?"

"Okay. Well. Just hand them over to me. Do you think I can't do it? I'll bring a bag or something."

I shook my head. I thought about it. I wondered if maybe the birds would attack him. The birds never pecked at me, but then again I had the food. I might have thought about giving Nate the birds after all, if I thought they'd get all mean and territorial on him.

Kids were still streaming in off the buses. I was usually the only bike rider. A couple of older kids walked by. I recognized them as friends of Sydney's brothers. It was Friday, so they wore their football jerseys to show school spirit. Fridays, the junior high school team played first, and then, under the lights, the varsity. We're too small to really have a junior varsity team. Once you're in high school, everybody's varsity.

Nate stuck out his chin and said hi to the two guys in jerseys. I wasn't surprised he knew them. Everybody was always waiting for Nate to get up to seventh grade so he could be on the football team.

One of the guys said to Nate, "You got soup for lunch today?"

"Yeah," the second guy said, "heard you're a soup fan, Emerling." They both smiled like they'd said something real smart.

Nate turned a hot and angry red, as scarlet as a Buckeye jersey. I didn't really catch on that they were talking about that rumor about his father. And then when I did, I didn't really mind. I know I should have. But at least Nate was done talking to me about filching some birds.

"Did you hear the one about the guy who swims in soup? No? I can't remember. Was it tomato soup?"

"Nah, man," the second kid said, "it was chicken soup,

right? All those little noodles scared him right out of town."

Nate's face was still red but he squared himself up and fixed his backpack straps again and got his jaw all tight and he didn't say a word to anybody, not even me. I asked Daniel about it later after we were both out in a game of Horse at recess. The soup story about Nate's dad. He was the one who told me about it the first time, but I thought it was a joke so I hadn't paid much attention. Daniel said it was true. He whispered loudly, "Don't let Nate hear you."

Homer showed up then. "What are you talking about?"

Daniel told him. He still whispered, but he was grinning the whole time. Homer laughed so loud he snorted.

"Shhh!" Daniel spit as he hissed at him.

"No way," Homer said. "That's the best story I've ever heard. Swimming in the soup."

"It wasn't the actual soup," Daniel said, "it was the water that was going to be turned into soup."

Homer was still laughing. "Whatever. That's pretty funny. It's *awesome*."

Daniel said, "I'd relax about it, if I were you, Homer."

He said, "My name's not Homer."

Homer ate lunch with us almost all the time, and he was Homer now for sure, for good, forever.

"Fact of life," Daniel said, shrugging.

"The soup story makes no sense," I told them. "How did he even get into the soup?"

"I said it was the water!"

If it had happened, there would have been a recall. My mom would have taken every can out of the house and back to the grocery store, and she would have called the company up and complained and they would have sent her a boatload of coupons.

"It could never happen. Wouldn't someone see you? Aren't there security cameras? Wouldn't you die in an industrial accident?"

"Nope. Because the guy—well, you know, same color as tomato soup," Homer said. Daniel said he was going to throw up and Homer laughed some more.

Tyler showed up and punched Daniel's arm. "It's not true," he said. He made a face at Homer. "It's not."

"Sure it's true," Daniel said.

"It's not."

Abby was with him. "It's just some rumor," she said. "No food place would ever let that happen."

"Yeah," Tyler said, "it's an urban legend. Guy swims in soup."

"It's not an urban legend," Homer said to Tyler and Abby, crossing his arms in a way that signaled he thought he was going to make some kind of really excellent point.

"You calling me a liar?"

Homer said, *"Au contraire.* You're not a liar. You're just wrong. This place is country. Urban means city. We don't have any such thing as urban legends."

The group broke up, except for me and Homer. He looked at me. "That's an *awesome* story."

"It's not that awesome," I said. I knew why he liked it. It was obvious why he liked it.

"I'm going to call him something. Nate. Mr. Soup, maybe."

"That's not a good idea."

"Why not? You're Itch. I'm Homer. I don't know why he can't be Mr. Soup."

"It doesn't work like that."

The game of Horse had started up again. Tyler, Daniel, Nate, Sydney, and Abby were playing. Abby missed and said she thought the game shouldn't be Horse. It should be a longer word. "Hippopotamus," she said.

"It's funny," Homer continued. "The guys will think it's funny." When I shook my head, Homer said, "You're just against it because he's your friend."

"That's not it."

"But he is your friend. And he calls you Itch."

"That's not why you can't call him Mr. Soup. I'm just telling you, I'm just letting you know, it doesn't work like that."

"Well, it should." Homer kicked at the crumbly playground blacktop.

I shrugged.

"My mom says I'm a stickler," Homer said. "You know, for the rules. Protocol. How things are done. So I don't get why you have a different name and I have a different name, and nobody's calling Daniel Chrome Dome and no one calls Nate Mr. Soup."

"Because it doesn't work that way."

Homer watched me for a while. Then he said, "I thought you'd be on my side. I thought you'd be on my team."

As soon as he said the word *team*, my brain started firing with all the ways I didn't like it and how he was wrong, how no way after spending three years learning to speak Buckeye and, you'd think finally, this year, no longer being the new kid, was I going to let Homer divvy up the class and put me on his side.

"I mean," Homer went on, "since we're the allergy kids—"

"I'm not allergic to anything. It's not an allergy." It bugged me that he didn't know the difference. Mr. Stickler.

"—and since we've got the nicknames."

"They're not for teams," I said. "We're not on the same team. There's no team."

"I'm just trying to fit in," he said.

"Yeah, well, that's not how you do it."

Homer was quiet for a minute, and I desperately hoped he wasn't going to ask me how he was supposed to fit in, because I did not know the answer. Sometimes I think it's just dumb luck, or magic, or just not having a body that betrays you, which is all the same thing.

"There are so teams," he said.

"What?"

"Itch. There are teams. Of course there are teams. I mean, why else would you put up with being called *Itch*? Because if you complain, you're afraid you'll get kicked off."

I stared at him. "You're *Homeschool* Homer. How much do you really know about school?"

"School's weird, that's what I know." He was worked up. He stood squared up with me and waved his arms. "You don't want to be on my team because you're scared you won't be on their team. If we all had nicknames, though, it'd be different."

"Don't mess with it," I told him, backing away from his flailing arms. "It's not about nicknames." I rode my bike with Nate. We played ball at the storage units. I got dizzy on the tire swing with the other guys. We all ate lunch together.

He huffed at me. "There's power in numbers."

I'd given up saying anything. I didn't know what to say.

"Think about it," he said. Then he ran over to the

basketball hoop and announced that Horse should be called Giganotosaurus because it was two letters longer than Hippopotamus.

It stayed Horse.

Back in the classroom after recess it took us a while to get quiet. Rustling coats and scraping chairs and kids still catching their breaths. Mrs. Anderson returned our math homework and, after a while, we settled down, and the only sound was the click of her shoes across the tile floor and the sound of papers rustling like dry leaves.

She returned our work facedown. Like it's a surprise. Like you can't read the grade and her comments, backward, through the paper.

I didn't even need to see the backward number to know it was lousy. I knew when I turned it in. There was an extra note too, written in cursive.

Sydney had been right to warn me.

The note said *See me*. Mrs. Anderson hit the first side of my homework hard—lots of red lines and corrections—but close to the bottom she drew a line and a note. "Too many errors to correct. Please come and see me."

I saw Nate's paper. His pencil lines were heavy and dark, like if he was going to get the assignment done he was going to take down the paper and pencil while he was at it. Eighty percent. *Eighty. Nate.*

"Yes!" he shouted, holding up his paper for the whole class to look at.

"That's a B-minus," Homer said, and you could tell he was never going to be impressed with a B-minus. I didn't used to be either.

"Yes! It's a B-minus! And," Nate said, "this is how I did it." He conked his head down onto the math book on his desk. He closed his eyes. He fake snored.

Homer said, "I don't get it."

Nate fake snored louder.

"I sleep with my books under my pillow."

Homer snorted, and Nate said, "It's called osmosis. Don't knock it."

Homer told him it didn't work that way.

We all quieted down when Mrs. Anderson returned to the front of the room. "If you're lost today, you'll be lost tomorrow." She stood at the blackboard and reminded us to raise our hands and ask when we had questions. Then she looked around the room and glanced right over me and I knew she really meant, *Mr. Fitch, you're lost.*

"So here's the plan," she announced. "I'm putting you in study groups this week. You will help each other learn. If you understand what you're doing, you'll learn even more by explaining it. If you don't understand what you're doing, well, maybe it's me. Maybe you'll understand it better if someone else explains it to you."

Daniel mumbled something about calculators. Mrs. Anderson read through a list. She put us in groups of three. She separated Nate and Daniel, which is what every teacher does, always. Nate got to work with Sydney, who is my secret math weapon. Daniel was in a group with Abby. Abby rolled her eyes. Tyler got a couple of girls.

Then Mrs. Anderson came to my group. "Mr. Fitch, Mr. Bishop, and Mr. Mott." That's me, Homer, and Lucas.

Homer was all about teams again. He wanted us to have a name. We changed seats and pushed desks together, and he was all, "Let's call ourselves the Common Denominators," and Lucas said he didn't think we had to come up with a name.

That didn't stop Homer. "Team Fraction?"

Lucas said, "The Fractured Fractions?"

"That doesn't sound very teamlike."

Lucas said, "It wasn't supposed to. It was a joke."

"Because we're not a team," I said. "We don't need a name."

Mrs. Anderson asked us if we were working hard or hardly working. We opened our books and I realized that both Homer (no surprise there) and Lucas knew what they were doing, and this group was all for me.

PS. In the math book, there was a problem about a pizza concession stand and leftovers and it had pictures of different kinds of pizzas. Round pizzas.

Lucas's notebook was a mess of numbers, fractions, and pictures, all smudged gray, matching the gray that always smeared the pinky side of his writing hand. He had drawings of helicopters and smoke and snakes and squiggles, and he gave some of his numbers faces. Eights had googly eyes. Sevens got hats. Some of the nines had arms and they pointed at the other numbers. If a number was double digit, he drew them arm-wrestling. Homer's eyes bugged at all the drawings. "Mrs. Anderson accepts that?"

"Yup."

Mrs. Anderson might not have looked me in the eye when she spoke about getting help, but my group was the first one she sat down with to go through our homework. It wasn't that I didn't get it. I did. But it was temporary. It was like memorizing something for a test—spelling words, or labeling the US states on a map—and at the time, in class, it didn't seem so bad. I'd get them right. I'd peek at my notes or the map once or twice. I thought I knew it because I'd looked. But I didn't know anything. I let it slide right out of my brain. And so when I'd get home I'd forget all the stuff Lucas and Homer had helped me with.

Once Mrs. Anderson went to work with the next group, Homer said, "Hey, Itch, I'll help you after school."

"I don't know," I told him.

"Maybe I could go to your house?"

"Sydney and I usually study together. And I've got a job too. I'm busy."

"Sydney can be there too. We could be a supergroup," he said. Then he sighed. "I'm not talking about being your friend. It's your math. Don't you want help with your math? I mean, I get it. You don't like me. But your math. You can get better."

"It's just math," I said. "My parents are both engineers. I can handle fractions."

"Well, I'd think you'd get it already then. I mean, you can't be an engineer if you get stuck on sixth-grade math."

As if I'd ask Homer for help. It would be like some cartoon. Itch and Homer. No way. "You can if you're in the sixth grade."

CHAPTER 10

ONCE IN A while we ate lunch outside at the picnic tables near the parking lot. We watched the high school seniors, who could leave school for lunch, come and go. Some drove off, but it was a long way to the nearest fast-food place. This is the country, remember. Most of the seniors walked to the gas station, which sold the bad pizza and slushies and hot dogs, and hung out in the parking lot.

I can tell if something is cold just by looking at it. I don't have to touch it. I can just look at it, and then I itch. It's that easy. So I can tell you, from twenty feet away, I knew those shaded picnic tables were going to be cold. I knew I was going to sit down on the cold bench and between the cold and the pressure of me just sitting—only sitting—the itch would crawl out of me and run down my legs, up my back, anywhere it could get to—which would be everywhere—and I'd have to spend all of lunch either wanting to scratch or scratching.

The wind didn't help. It was like an extra hand on my skin.

When I didn't sit down, one of the lunch ladies came over and told me to park it. Because we still had lunch ladies.

Sydney asked, "What are you eating, Isaac?"

"An air sandwich," I said. "Want the recipe?"

Taking apart my two slices of bread, I gave each one a little wave. I looked at Nate, because I knew he would laugh. "Freshening it up."

He thought it was pretty funny. I was glad. It was good to make him laugh after I'd annoyed him about not getting him a bird. I was relieved. I might have laughed too, but all I could think about was not itching. So far I was following my rules. No itching. No witnesses. But every time I stopped myself from itching the wind kicked up and did it for me.

Homer said, "That's rude."

"What's rude?"

"Flapping your bread."

"You mean like table manners?"

"No, not like table manners. You're rude because you're flaunting it."

My face got hot and the back of my neck felt even itchier and I wanted to scratch at it but didn't dare while Homer was after me about table manners. "I don't get it."

"You're waving your empty sandwich around."

Sydney said, "It's two slices of bread. It's not a sandwich."

Homer said, "You're making a big deal out of not eating peanut butter, and everybody knows that peanut butter is your favorite food."

"It's not," I told him. "I'm not. And I'm not breaking the rules. I'm not eating peanut butter. I'm doing a good thing here."

"Like it's so hard to find something to eat," Homer said. "Everybody else has managed it."

Sydney was busy polishing an apple with her shirt and so she wasn't looking at me. I thought about the day of the tornado and my lucky-not-lucky peanut shell. I'd showed it to Sydney. I told her it was my good-luck charm. I told her it worked for her too, but she laughed and said it was her own power and my house that got her to safety.

"I've got muscles," she said. "I didn't need luck from a peanut shell."

What if Homer was right? Was I being a jerk, flapping my bread around? Before, he was all about helping me out with math and now he was sneering at me and my air sandwich. Maybe he'd decided to stick with his idea of teams, after all, and I wasn't on his.

Anyway, the guys were laughing and I decided I wasn't going to worry about Homer.

What started at lunch couldn't be stopped. Even the not-coolness of the classroom was no relief because just warming up became its own kind of itching. All I wanted was to itch. Itch until I burned and it felt better and worse at the same time and then itch some more.

The next thing I knew, I heard Daniel say, "There he goes again," and Mrs. Anderson volunteered Homer to escort me to the nurse's office.

Was Mrs. Anderson kidding me? Was she trying to make this worse? "No," I said, "no, thank you. I know the way."

That made the class laugh. I rubbed my hand across my face. My cheeks burned and prickled.

"Mr. Bishop. Please escort Mr. Fitch to the nurse's office." Everybody laughed some more. Everybody except Homer. And Sydney. But then, thanks to that swipe across my face, my eyelids were puffing up and maybe I wasn't seeing things clearly. "I'll call the nurse to let her know you're on your way." Mrs. Anderson handed me my backpack and sweatshirt.

Walking was going to be murder.

And no way was I going to put on my backpack.

I wasn't going to let that beast out. Not any farther.

Homer closed the classroom door so quietly behind us

you would have thought the whole place was filled with sleeping babies, not kids talking about dogs with no fur and bloated fish on the beach.

"So you've got it now. The itch."

"Yeah."

"Is it going to be bad?"

I tried to be like Mr. Epple. I didn't want to give him any words.

"Well?"

"No."

"Oh."

"Do you want it to be bad?" Because he sounded like watching me itch would be really interesting.

"Of course not."

"Because it's not going to be bad. It's going to be nothing." I stopped walking. I had to stop.

"Look at your hands," Homer said. "They are amazing. They look like raw hamburger meat."

"It's not amazing. It's the total opposite of amazing." I didn't need to look at my hands to know they were splotchy and red.

Homer stood with me, his back against the smooth blue tile wall near the first-grade classrooms. The hallways always made me think of a swimming pool.

Homer handed me some papers from the teacher. "It looks like she's already assembled your homework."

Grabbing the papers, I told Homer, "I'm not going home."

"Get better, not bitter."

"I've heard." When I shoved the papers into my bag, the box with my peanut shell fell out.

It was a hard black cardboard cube. Tiny gold dots lined the edges. The top of the box had a small strap and a snap to close it. The lid opened up in the middle like two doors, and inside it was white and cushiony.

"What's that?"

"A box," I said. I got that hot taste in my mouth, the one right before you throw up. It had nothing to do with itching. "Hey! Don't touch it!" I swatted his hand away.

"It looks like a little coffin."

It was all over then. The beast was out. Even standing there with Homer by the first-grade classrooms, I was ready to itch myself inside out and upside down.

"Oh, wow. Itch. You should see your face."

Until that moment, I thought I could fight the itch. I thought it was possible. That's what my lucky peanut shell habit gave me. But then in the hallway I wondered. What if as something changed on the outside of my body, something changed deep inside me too? What if fighting the itch was pointless because I really was the itch? What if it really was goodbye, Isaac Fitch, and hello, Itch?

When we got to the nurse's office, Homer filled the nurse in with all the details, right down to my hamburger hands. He sounded like a TV doctor and made hamburger hands sound like a real thing.

The school nurse had a lot of dark hair she wore in a bun on the top of her head. It was the size of a cake. She always wore white. She looked like she'd been there since the school was built, which was before my parents were born. It's one of those buildings that was supposed to look new forever but then was just ugly.

"Hey, buddy," she said, like we were old friends. Maybe we were. Maybe it was pretty memorable, in a day full of stomachaches and throw-up, when I came in. "I'm going to give you one of your antihistamines, okay?" She brought me a small paper cup of water that turned soggy while I held it and dug into her locked box of medicines until she found mine—sealed up in a plastic bag with paperwork stapled to it.

As I chewed the purple pill, Homer said, "That's it? Your whole body transforms and all you need is an over-the-counter allergy pill from the drugstore?" He didn't close his mouth when he was done talking. That's how surprised he was. Or disappointed.

The nurse said, "I'll call your mom."

I told the nurse my mom was in China.

Homer wished me good luck before he left, and I lay on the crinkly paper cover of the bed in the nurse's office. I could see through the windows that looked out to the front of the school. I held perfectly still, arms out, legs apart. The itch didn't stop. The medicine would take about an hour to work. I stared up at the ceiling. My dad always told me that when he had nothing to do but stare at the ceiling he counted the holes or dots or whatever in it. Or he found patterns. Or he counted the dots on each square and then counted each square and figured out how many dots were on the whole ceiling.

He's the kind of person who could do that in about thirty seconds.

I thought about my latest emails with Mom. She wrote me that she always liked school cheeseburgers. She wrote me a story about someone she knew who ate a hard-boiled egg every day. They boiled one egg a day and it had to be perfect. If it wasn't perfect the person wouldn't eat it. I typed, *Was it you?* She wrote, *Not me. Boiling only a single egg is inefficient.* But I could only not itch and think about eggs and perfection and China and ceilings for so long.

I started thinking about Sydney. I started thinking about Sydney and lunch. How she didn't say anything when Homer said I was rude. She usually stood up for herself. But this time she must have known I was fighting the itch. She knew I was going to balloon into the beast. She was being nice. She wasn't going to get into a big argument with me and Homer over my air sandwich while I was trying not to itch. But maybe she agreed with Homer? I didn't want her to be nice. If I hurt her, I wanted to know.

After a while I pointed to the windows and told the nurse, "My dad's coming in. Can I go?" I wanted to say, *I'm going, I'm gone, goodbye.*

"Sure," she said, the hair cake bobbing. She probably thought I was going to meet my dad in the office while he signed me out. "Take care of yourself, okay, buddy?"

The school's heavy front doors clunked closed behind me but I kept my cool. I knew how bad I looked. No one was going to stop me. I grabbed my bike and rode out to the farm.

It was harder than I thought it would be. The medicine was starting to make me sleepy. My hands were so swollen I couldn't get them all the way around the handlebars. My helmet made my head itch so I took it off.

Scraping my teeth against my tongue, I decided it felt normal. Not swollen. I took a big gulp of air, just to check. Stretched out my lungs. Everything still worked, on the inside. I wasn't going to die out here on a country road, at least not from idiopathic angioedema.

At the farm, Mr. Epple's truck was gone. A thin day-time moon shone in the clear blue sky. There wasn't a soul around. It felt good. I didn't have to have a name. The wind rustled the high, yellowing grass. The birds called and their wings *drum-drum-drummed*. They scuttled all around me when I went in to feed them. I missed Brutus.

It wasn't long before my dad found me. He didn't even shut the car door when he got out, just charged into the pen, and the pheasants all around me chucked and called and ran to hide in the scrub.

"Isaac! Isaac!"

He'd never hit me before. He was close now, but once he got a good look at me he stopped moving. His clenched-up mad hand stuck out unmoving in front of him. That's how I knew for sure how ugly and red and swollen I was.

"Isaac." He said it quietly. Then he marched up, grabbed my ear, and started to drag me off.

"Wait! Wait! I've got to shut it up right and lock it."

"Oh, for Pete's sake." He let go of me. He looked differ-ent with his beard. Madder. More serious. Bigger. Maybe he really would hit me.

After I secured the pens, he shoved me in the back seat

of the car, cop-style, and we drove off. I didn't tell him we'd left my bike behind.

We were quiet as we drove past the ditch I had crashed in, the school, the buses starting to line up, Nate's grandmother's storage units, the long straight street where we lived and where Ohio State flags snapped in the wind. My hands still looked like raw hamburger.

CHAPTER 11

I FELL ASLEEP AFTER we got home. Dad woke me up before dinner and set his laptop on my bed and said Mom wanted to talk to me. It was six a.m., China time.

Mom was frozen in a slow-connection smile and that's why I didn't like to see her, stuck, her face blurring out. Her second night of the trip we'd tried this and I hated it.

Her picture jerked to life again and filled in with detail, but when she said, "Your father and I just had an interesting discussion," she sounded as though her voice was coming through pipes under the ocean.

"Okay," I said. No surprise there.

"Dad talked to your doctor. You're getting some new medicine. You can take the pills every day to keep things under control."

"Are they going to put me to sleep?"

"What? I didn't hear you."

I leaned over to the laptop's mic and said it again. Mom said they weren't supposed to make me drowsy. "You take one pill every day and then one if you feel itchy. You don't have to wait for the hives and everything."

"Am I grounded?"

She sounded human and not so far away when she answered. "Of course you're grounded. Work and school. And you're lucky to keep work, young man."

She didn't say anything about the terms for my job at the farm, which meant her conversation with Dad wasn't as interesting as it could have been. It meant Dad didn't tell her about my math homework. Because Dad knew. He'd found it crumpled up on the basement stairs right after we'd gotten home from the farm. First he was upset about finding something on the stairs. "You'll trip and crack your head open. You know better." Then, "Isaac, you have to try." He'd opened the crumpled ball. "If you can't start doing better, then that's it. No more pheasant farm. Do we understand each other?" The real answer was no, we did not understand each other, but I told him yes.

Mom asked, "How's school going? How's math?"

I asked, "How am I supposed to do well in math if I can't go over to Sydney's to study?"

"Maybe your dad will let her come over. You can also go see your teacher for help. And ask Dad! He's right there. And I promise you, he can do any math problem you can throw at him."

"Ha. He can *do* the math but he's no good at waiting for *me* to figure out how to do it." But I liked the thought of literally throwing math problems at him, like they were ninja stars.

She froze again, her eyes half closed, her mouth open, like a bad photograph you'd delete right away. "I hate this," I said. "This doesn't work."

I thought I'd lost the connection, but Mom was still there. "Love you!"

While Mom is gone, Dad and I play Spit. We don't do math together. I don't ask him. He doesn't ask me.

I used to play it with Sydney until her life got busy.

Spit is a two-person card game. It's the kind of game that can get rough. So me and Dad, we're always slapping hands and waving arms and sometimes we knock heads. It's the kind of card game that counts as exercise.

When I first taught it to Sydney on my front porch, I didn't tell her part of the objective was speed. It didn't matter. She rose up on her knees and started slamming down cards, and when she beat me she hollered and waved her arms and the tail of her braid whipped across my eyes and I couldn't open them for ten minutes.

"Sorry! Sorry!" She was laughing, though, so it didn't sound sincere.

I had my hand over my eyes. Tears ran down my cheeks.

"I'm really sorry, you know." She put her hand on my shoulder and crouched in front of me. "Can you really not open them?"

I nodded.

"Well," she said, starting to laugh again, "maybe you deserve it. You know, for tricking me."

"Maybe," I told her. "But maybe not. Man, that braid is lethal."

"Yeah," she said, "that's what I've got it for."

"Nate didn't catch on nearly as fast."

She snorted. "I think he's been drinking the green river water."

The late bus stopped down the street from my house, and usually these days Sydney waved and kept running.

Today she hollered "Isaac!" her hand up in a wave, her backpack banging behind her, her cleats clicking on the sidewalk. She wore tie-dyed-looking orange knee socks and her legs were splattered with mud. When my parents wouldn't let me sign up for football, Sydney tried to get me to sign up for soccer instead. She said maybe my parents would let me be a kicker. She said plenty of football kickers got their start in soccer. I got the job on the pheasant farm instead.

She shouted as she ran closer. "Hey! Do you want to

do our math together? Come over tomorrow." She stopped running and took two walking strides, her hands at her hips, kicking through the yellow maple leaves I'd have to rake later. "You okay?"

Was Homer right about the things he'd said about my air sandwich? And had Sydney let me off the hook because she knew I was getting itchy? Can she tell when I'm going to turn into the beast? I didn't ask her about any of that.

I asked, "Do you ever wish it would go away? Your allergies? Don't you wish it would just stop?"

Just like that, everything about her changed. Standing on the sidewalk at the bottom of my front steps, she wilted. Her happy-to-see-me, on-the-run face melted into something sad. She looked tired from soccer. Seeing her like that, sad and still and tired, felt private and at the same time big and obvious. Maybe it was something I should have already seen. "Sure," she said, "of course I do. Don't you wish your itch would go away?"

"It's not the same. It's just a...a...thing. It's not life-threatening. It doesn't mean I have to raise my hand any-time somebody is checking to see if someone has an allergy and it doesn't mean I can't eat the birthday cupcakes or the pizza for the class party, and it doesn't mean I can't go out and get Chinese food." Just thinking about it put a pinch in my chest. "It doesn't mean what's regular for everybody else is poison for me."

"Yeah," she said quietly, "it stinks." She dropped down onto the first step and slumped into her backpack. "Sometimes it's a long line of stink with some terror thrown in."

"Do you think Homer was right about my air sandwich? Am I being a jerk?"

"Yes. No. I don't know. I mean, I know how hard it is to get the right food all the time, so I kind of just want to leave you alone about it, but living without peanut butter for a few months really isn't that big of a deal."

"Right."

She shrugged. "I don't know. It's a peanut-eat-peanut world. A peanutty, sesame seedy, cheesy world. And that's just the stuff that *I'm* allergic to." She sighed. "Have you ever noticed how much dairy is in the world? And peanuts on *everything*? And don't even get me started on hummus."

"Hummus?"

She waved a hand. "It's got mashed sesame seeds in it, except it's called tahini."

"I didn't know that."

She shrugged.

I told her, "I like the food you eat. Your mom's cookies? The best ever."

"I mean, the world is practically cheese-covered. Totally

disgusting, revolting cheese. Just orangey, melty cheese and moldy cheese and gloppy yogurt. And then people mix peanuts into it. Ugh."

"Yeah. What's up with cottage cheese?" I was trying to make her laugh. "And, and, *headcheese*?"

"Itch," she said, "that's not cheese, it's brains."

"Oh. Then for sure I'm definitely not eating it. So, um, it's good to know Homer now, right? Because he gets it? What it's really like to have food allergies?" It killed me to say it, but I figured it was the truth and I owed her at least that much. What if there really *were* teams in school, and Sydney ended up on Homer's team instead of mine?

"Sure, it's nice. Homer's a good guy. But he's still not my best friend or anything." She pulled her orange socks up to her knees. She was ready to run the rest of the way home.

"About the math? You'll have to come here. I'm grounded."

"For how long?"

"For forever."

"How about we study during lunch?"

"I can do that."

She asked, "You're grounded for Saturday's game too?"

"Yeah, Saturday too."

"Rough," she said, and then she was running again

and was past my house. She looked back over her shoulder. "Watch out, fractions!"

The next day, Sydney and I slipped away from our class as we were herded to the auditorium for lunch, turning down the hallway and past the hanging sheets of clear plastic that surrounded the wrecked cafeteria. Drills whirred and there was some banging, and in the distance a radio played. We went to a little dead-end hallway past the empty band room and sat on the floor near an exit.

We sat cross-legged, and Sydney ate a SunButter sandwich. I didn't have an air sandwich. I ate a jelly sandwich, no peanut butter, no SunButter, and it wasn't any good. It was soggy and too sweet. We balanced our open math books on our knees. "It's just a lot of little math problems inside one big one," she said, before reading through a word problem about how humans sleep for a third of each day and then figuring out the number of days the average person sleeps in a year.

"It says a year is three hundred sixty-five and one-quarter days," I said. *"One-quarter.* Now they're just trying to make it extra hard."

"Come on!" She knocked her shoulder into mine. Then she asked, "Are you going to tell me why you're grounded?"

I shrugged. She wouldn't like hearing that I'd skipped

school. Not even Nate would do that. I only told her I went out to the farm without my dad's permission. I left out everything else, including how yesterday after school I walked out to the farm because we'd left my bike there.

The floor was cold and dusty. As Sydney went through the next problem about yards of fabric, I rubbed the pink pencil eraser over the back of my hand. Erase, erase, erase, scrub, scrub, scrub, until my hand was under a snow of pink flecks.

Sydney grabbed my arm. "What are you *doing*?"

"Not paying attention?"

"Yeah, that's obvious, but look at your hand. You're itching."

"Math makes me itch."

She rolled her eyes. "Don't you have medicine? Doesn't your mom give you medicine or call the doctor's office, or—" She stopped, brushing all the pink eraser pieces off my notebook. "Sorry. I forgot about China."

I shrugged. "It's okay. It's not like I'm a baby. I can take my own medicine."

"Yeah, but you *don't*."

"It's not like it's a guarantee. It's not like it always works."

She shook her head. Her face was tight. Frowning. "Okay, look, you know how me or my parents always carry my epinephrine? Two injectors, all the time, like you're supposed to carry? Even when I'm not going to eat anything? Somebody always has them because what's the point of having lifesaving medication if you don't have it with you?"

"My medicine isn't lifesaving. My life's not in danger. It's just a thing."

"But if you never take it, it will never work."

She closed the math book. The pages flipped closed like a fan, sending even more of the eraser pieces flying. "Seriously, Isaac, maybe you should figure this out. The medicine part, not the fractions."

"You're a lousy math tutor."

She glared at me instead of laughing. After a while she said, "I'm better than your dad."

"For sure." My dad was too brilliant to explain basic math because to him it was like telling someone how to breathe. If you ever try to explain breathing or think too hard about it, you only end up in worse shape than before because you're not supposed to think about it. That's how it is for my dad. "You're not as good as my mom, though."

"Yeah. The unit test is before Halloween. Will she be back before then?"

"Probably not. I don't know." My hands were streaked with red. Probably just from the erasing. Probably I could leave it alone. Probably I could not itch. Probably I wouldn't need to go to the nurse. "It would be nice, though."

We talked about Halloween for a little while, about how she was pretty sure she was going to be a zombie. She said she thought I should be a pheasant, which I thought was dorky. And complicated. "How would I even get a costume like that?" Anyway, I was grounded.

"Just start collecting feathers." She grinned. It was a joke. "Hey," she said, "I heard you're going to get Nate a bird."

CHAPTER 12

EVERYBODY WAS TALKING about birds and the farm the next day at lunch.

Tyler asked, "Aren't there emus back there? Or ostriches?"

We were back in the art room. As the school year went on, it got stinkier and stinkier. Paint. Glue. Fat Magic Markers. If my mom weren't in China, she'd investigate and warn that we might be eating in a room filled with toxic fumes.

Nate said, "They're pheasants. Emus are something else altogether. Emus are big. You can ride an emu."

Tyler snorted. "Is that true?"

"That old farmer won't miss a bird," said Daniel.

"He will if it's an emu," Sydney said.

I was done with air sandwiches. I ate a strawberry jam and cream cheese sandwich with some green pepper slices on the side. I was done with the peanut shell too. I dumped it out of its box into the garbage and put the box on my mother's dresser. It had never worked. It was just a thing

I'd carried around. And I felt bad for ever showing the shell to Sydney.

"He'll miss a bird," I said. "That's the whole point. Counting the birds, the eggs, and then the chicks. That's how he makes money."

Lucas asked, "How does he make money from birds?"

Sydney answered. "He sells them."

"For pets?" Homer asked. "I'd rather have a dog."

"For hunts," I said. "Mostly."

"That's not fair," said Homer.

Nate said, "I want a bird." He pointed at me. "I want two birds."

Lucas turned to me, asking, "What do you mean, for hunts?"

"He sells the pheasants to private preserves. Private land where you can hunt whenever you want, or something. The pheasants live there, and people pay to go hunting, to get a chance to shoot a pheasant."

"Seriously?" Homer asked. "Who does that?"

"Don't look at me," Nate said. "I just hunt deer. Well, and squirrel. But squirrels don't count. They're more like target practice. Got to get ready, you know. Youth deer-gun season starts weekend before Thanksgiving. That's like, four weeks away." Nate was casual about it, but I bet he was crossing out the days on his calendar.

Homer asked, "But would you do such a thing? If you could? Would you pay to go hunting birds that are sitting there just for you to kill?"

Daniel said, "Don't be stupid, Homer. They're birds. They can fly away."

Nate said, "I'd do it if I could bag a lion. That would be *sweet.*"

"Not if it's easy. Not if it's right there waiting. That's not fair."

"It's not *easy.* It's a skill. You have to be *patient.* My grandpa and me—we get up earlier than I do for school and plan where to go, and track, or sit out in a tree stand somewhere for hours, *hours,* and then you have to know what you're doing, it's not just dumb luck." Then Nate asked Homer, "Don't you hunt? Weren't you home-schooled? I thought homeschoolers were all survivalists and stuff."

Homer shook his head. "You just sit in a tree? And wait for some deer to walk by?"

"Yeah."

"And then you kill it?"

"Yeah. And then I eat it."

Nate grinned. We laughed. Homer was horrified. "That's *atrocious,*" he hissed.

Daniel asked, "How can this be news to you?"

"It's the food chain," Sydney said. "Do you eat cow? How's it any different with a cow?"

By the next day's lunch we were on a whole new topic. We were in the gym. Everybody was busy telling Homer about how last year an eighth-grader stole frog legs from the biology lab and stuck them in the salad bar. It was a good story. Funny and disgusting at the same time. The kid who did it was the smartest kid in the whole eighth grade. He wanted to be a doctor. They said that was how the biology teacher figured it out, because the cuts on the legs were so good. Also, since he normally wasn't a troublemaker, he confessed quickly.

The gym was my favorite place to eat. We could be as loud as we wanted. When you were done eating, you could play basketball. Mr. Mullins didn't like it. He came out of his office every now and then and crossed his arms and scowled at us, probably thinking about all the ways our food could ruin his nice gym floor.

Tyler said he'd never confess, not like the kid who took the frog legs. "If you're smart," he said, "you know what you can get away with."

"Nuh-uh," Sydney said. "If you're smart, you know what you *can't* get away with."

Dad had made me a roast beef sandwich. I think it was supposed to be special. I hate roast beef. I like it for dinner but not cold and soft like cloth in a sandwich. I ate a slice of bread.

Daniel leaned over and asked if he could have the meat. "You're weird, man. Who doesn't want roast beef? It's the best lunch meat you're ever going to get. It's classy." He dangled the whole piece above his mouth and then dropped it in. He didn't wait to finish chewing before he said, "Too many air sandwiches, Itch. They went to your head."

Homer, who had looked appalled at the way Daniel had stuffed his face, suddenly thought what Daniel had said was especially funny, which bothered me more than any- thing Daniel said because it was just Daniel being Daniel.

Homer laughed and laughed about what Daniel had said about air sandwiches and my brain. I could see his teeth—skinny, like the rest of him, and with a lot of space between each one—and I realized maybe he'd figured out a way to fit in. Maybe it was to laugh at me.

Nate stood up on one of the bleachers and announced, "Let's take a vote. Who here thinks my friend Itch should get me a bird?"

It got about as quiet as it gets in a gym full of kids eat- ing lunch. All eyes were on me. I looked at my feet. I didn't want to see Homer's picket fence teeth or Nate's big grin.

"All in favor?" Everybody raised their hands. Kids spread out on the bleachers and far away from us. Abby and Maria. Lucas. Daniel and Tyler. No surprise there. Sydney. Homer. Guess we weren't on the same team, no matter what he said. And wouldn't you think he'd have issues with the morality and legality of stealing? Well, he didn't. He said it would be a good thing, saving a pheasant. He said he was glad Nate was turning into a lover, not a fighter, which made most of us pretend vomit.

The next day at lunch Homer showed me his sandwich, peeling back one slice of brown bread to show me what was inside.

"Air," he said. "It's an air sandwich." He whispered. As if we were friends with a secret.

"Hey, guys," I said, "look who's got an air sandwich!"

He stuck his chin forward and made a face. "It's because of what Sydney said about the cow. How I eat beef and don't even think about it."

"But you don't eat beef for lunch," Sydney said. "Right?"

"I usually had meat in my sandwich. Turkey. With mustard." He sighed. "But I couldn't stop thinking last night about how I thought it was cruel to shoot deer and then how I could eat turkey in my lunch."

"You could just be happy," Nate said, "that you're at the top of the food chain." He took a big bite of his sandwich. He'd told us earlier it was roadkill.

"My mom was going to send soup," Homer said quietly. "In a thermos." He looked at me.

"Not a good idea," I whispered. It would have been too mean not to keep him straight with this. To let him think it would be okay to bring in soup. It would be like poking a bear, and the bear was Nate.

"I know." Then he leaned toward me. He whispered too. "What am I supposed to do? Cut out a whole category of food?"

Nate didn't look at him. If he heard us talking about soup he wasn't going to show it. If the big kids didn't bother him, then Homer wasn't even a blip on his radar.

"That's funny, Homer," I said, "because the answer is yes."

"My name's not *Homer*. And it's not like I can pick my lunch from all the foods, Itch. You can pick from *all the foods*."

"Yeah, well, my name's not *Itch* either."

Sydney said, "I like sunflower seed butter. My mom says she likes it better than peanut butter too, and she can eat anything."

Homer nodded. "I was in a hurry. I needed something fast, so I thought, oh, yeah, air sandwich."

Everyone went back to their lunches. They didn't care. Homer took a bite. "It's good."

I guess Homer wasn't too mad at me for calling out his air sandwich because the next day I found an invitation from him in my desk. Flat and uncrumpled and totally out of place.

The envelope was red. Square. Inside was a fancy, thick card, red too, but not really red—officially it was scarlet. I knew this because there was a big *O* for Ohio State on the cover with two little buckeye leaves down in the *O*'s right corner.

The room was filled with the sound of ripping paper and before long kids were saying, "Cool!" and "Wow, Homer, cool!" Tyler got some high fives because he was wearing an Ohio State jersey. Once a kid had a whole-class birthday party at a bowling alley, but this was definitely going to be the coolest party we'd ever been to.

It was a neat trick. Everyone forgot all about Homer's concern for emus and the food chain.

Homer had a smile stretched all across his face. "We'll watch the game outside! We project it right onto the side of the house! Don't worry about the weather because we have heat lamps!"

Daniel asked, "Why isn't the bus going to be at the game? Why would you be *here* when you could be *there*?"

Homer said something about the bus getting old and

unreliable. Nate said "Yeah," in the way that didn't mean yeah. Homer told Nate, "It will be the next-best thing to being there."

"Maybe," Nate said. "My dad said he's going to take me next season."

Daniel said, "Your dad. Right."

"Shut up about it," Nate said, rising out of his chair.

I didn't really think the chicken noodle soup scared his dad out of town, but even so everybody knew Nate lived with his grandparents. They looked old too, like old grandparents, not young ones, and when they showed up at school events they looked like they stepped out of one of the historical photos that hung in the hall by the office. Homer laughed. I don't know why he laughed. Nate turned his angry gaze to him. "Don't worry," Homer said, smiling big in the face of Nate's scowl, "it's going to be awesome. I've been going to games and tailgating since I was a baby, and it's the tailgating that makes the game. Gives you the whole experience. I promise you, Nate, it's the next-best thing to being at the Shoe. We put down turf. Plus, we've got a projection TV like you won't believe." Homer yammered on about resolution and thousands upon thousands of pixels.

And wouldn't you know it, the invitation gave me a paper cut. It smarted. Blood welled up.

"You going?" Sydney asked me.

I couldn't believe I'd have to miss this. No one would ever think I was a Buckeye. Everybody would be there, and I'd be home, watching the game on TV. And that was if I was lucky. If I wasn't lucky, my dad would decide we had to go to the mall or something. This was crucial. It was big. No one in class would miss this. I'd be the only one who wasn't there.

"Sure." Maybe I could convince my dad.

Sydney grinned. "You're not grounded anymore?"

Instead of reminding her that I was grounded for an eternity, I showed her my blood. "Look at that. Scarlet. Just like yours."

Homer stuck his head over and said, "I don't see the gray." He turned to Sydney. "Can my mom call your mom and talk food?" I couldn't see Sydney's face, just the back of Homer's head. "Syd. Just think. It's my party and we can eat all the food."

When Homer finally moved I saw Sydney's smile. People say stuff like this all the time, but it was true: she lit up. That's how people say it. When someone looks so happy it's like there's something electric on the inside that gets turned on and shines out. "That sounds really cool, Homer."

Mom: *Do you need Dad's help with your math? Dad will help you.*

Me:

Mom: *What is that?*

Me: *Me and Dad doing math homework. You know how it is. He's too smart for fractions.*

Mom: *When's your math test?*

Me: *Next week.*

Mom: *Are you ready?*

Me: *Sydney helped me out. I think I got it. I'll be glad when we can get it over with and learn something else.*

Mom: *Good luck.*

Me: *Ha, ha, ha, you mean I don't have to study? I can just count on good luck?*

Mom: *It's a one-two approach. Preparedness. Finger-crossing. Preparedness first, of course.*

Was there an eye-roll emoji? I couldn't find an eye-roll emoji.

Mom: *Dad says you aren't taking your new medicine every day. It lasts longer and shouldn't make you*

sleepy. Take it every day to preempt an outbreak and
then take another if you do get one.
Me: *It just happens sometimes. And they taste awful.*

The flavor was supposed to be orange or lemon but instead it tasted like a metal-and-powdered-lemonade mix.

Mom: *I think you can handle it.*
Me: *Why can't I go to the football party at the Buckeye Bus? It's a once-in-a-lifetime opportunity. If you live in Ohio, it's against the law to forbid your kid to go to a football party. PS. Supervised by adults.*
Mom: *Not even going to answer that one.*
Me: *But it's not until November. Won't I get parole or anything? A weekend off?*
Mom: *Next topic, please.*
Me: *When are you coming home?*
Mom: *Soon. Keep those fingers crossed. Tell me more about school?*

I wrote back about the bird farm. Even though it was old news, I told her about Brutus and the owl. I asked what birds she'd seen. I sent her a picture of Dad's beard.
She answered right away. *Yowzers! Mountain man!*

CHAPTER 13

THE DAY OF our math test we got stuck having lunch in our own room, which is the worst. You don't have any long walk anywhere. You don't get a new place to sit. No change of scenery. You're just glued to your same old same old. We asked Mrs. Anderson if we could rearrange the desks and she said it was unnecessary, but she still got to go off to the teachers' lounge that always smelled like coffee and popcorn, and one of the lunch monitors came in and sat at her desk. The monitors were really the regular cafeteria workers, who had to do this until the cafeteria was finished. I think it was a pretty good job. This one sat at the desk and ate her bag lunch, read a book, and played with her phone.

Daniel was the first to move his desk and then everyone was doing it. Nate and Tyler. The girls who don't usually break any rules. Sydney swapped seats so she could sit in the back with Abby and Maria, her ballet friends, and talk about the Christmas show they were all in. Homer didn't move his desk. It sat there like an island.

My desk is always a mess and my math and social studies books slid out when I shoved over to Nate's desk. He wasn't my first-choice lunch partner, but we weren't re-arranging things entirely, just breaking out of the rows and lines we'd sat in all day. Homer leaned over and peered into my desk. "Nice," he said.

"Works for me," I said. "You use all your time orga-nizing and I use my time finding stuff. It's the same in the end."

"It kind of looks like a garbage can."

Nate thumped Homer on the back. "That's a normal sixth-grader's desk, Homer. You're just unfamiliar."

Homer didn't have anything to say to that and focused on setting up his lunch. He asked me if I was ready for the test.

"Sure," I said. I wasn't counting on a perfect score or anything, but something solid. Something that would make Mrs. Anderson forget she ever stopped grading my home-work because it was too messed up. And, I'm not going to lie, I wanted to beat whatever Nate's score was.

Because I was thinking about fractions, it took a minute for it to register that Homer had set up a silver thermos on his desk. I couldn't believe it.

"Homer!" I whisper-yelled. "What are you doing?"

"My mom packed my lunch."

"Come on! Aren't you old enough to pack your own lunch?"

He gave me a look. I guess he knew that half the time my dad made my lunch too. "She doesn't like that I gave up lunch meat."

"This isn't how you do it, you know." I didn't say this wasn't how you made friends, fit in, protected yourself. One way for sure not to do those things is to say any of them out loud.

"I know."

"Okay. Well, keep it under the radar. Eat fast."

He nodded and then poured some soup—tomato soup, of course it was tomato soup, the only thing that would have been worse would have been chicken noodle—into the lid that was also a cup and drank it and then ate some crackers.

Nate slapped his lunch down on the desk. First was a sandwich wrapped in waxed paper, like it had come from the past in a time machine. There might as well have been a sign on it: MADE BY GRANDMA. Next were two juice boxes, an apple, and a stack of cookies still in their plastic wrapping but that had mostly already crumbled into pieces.

Nate stared at Homer. "You planning on staying a skinny little dude your whole life?"

"What?" Homer bobbled the cup and the drops of the tomato soup on the desk looked like blood. We were all thinking it.

Daniel tried not to laugh. Tyler had trouble too. Nate breathed loudly and slowly the way I imagine a bear might when it's out of its cave and sees a person and it's just deciding that it's going to have that person for dinner.

"Nate." That was me. I don't know what made me want to distract Nate from Homer and his industrial-accident soup. We were still friends, even though I was still upset about the eggs and pheasants and stealing talk and all the times he'd called me *Itch*, but I said his name all the same. I knew what it was like. Maybe not the bear part. But I know that feeling *before*. Before it all falls apart. Before it all changes. Before the tornado. Before the itch takes over and the beast is out. Because right now, right now there's a chance to stop it and because I knew how things could go for Homer. "Nate. I got a salami sandwich. Can I trade you for one of yours?"

It took a minute but Nate said, "Sure, man," and I passed my sandwich over. Homer finished his soup like it was a contest and then he must have realized he was still hungry and Nate was at least a little bit right, because he kept studying all the food the rest of us had spread out.

When I peeled back the waxed paper I realized I'd gotten a rotten deal, because Nate had a bologna sandwich. Now it was mine. Bologna is disgusting. I hate it. Nate's sandwich also had a slice of smooth orange cheese that probably didn't even have to be refrigerated and was incapable of melting. The white bread was the kind that was so soft it was almost impossible to chew. Also, I actually like salami. Dad only bought it because Mom was away. He'd probably have to tear up the grocery store receipts, that's how much Mom hates salami. She says it's way too unhealthy and it will never be in our home. And I had a roll. Just to try something new. One of those nice round rolls that's kind of golden on top and there's a little bit of white flour on the bottom as though it's from a fancy bakery and not from a bag in the bread aisle of the grocery store. I had a roll, salami, and spicy mustard. For once, I had a good sandwich, and I went and traded it for a bologna and maybe-cheese sandwich that Nate's grandma packed a million years ago.

Next to me, Daniel had a lunch pack of two mini hot dogs, ketchup and mustard, juice, a chocolate bar, and some stubby carrot sticks. "Want to trade?"

He looked at the sandwich wrapped in waxed paper. "What is it?"

"It's bologna," I told him.

Nate said, "I'll trade with you, Daniel." Nate held up my salami sandwich.

"But we just switched!"

Nate shrugged. "It's mine now."

"Want to trade back?"

"Nah. But I'll trade Daniel."

Daniel's lunch was the best and we all knew it. Daniel said, "I'll trade for Tyler's cold pizza. Hot dogs and carrots only."

That's when Homer the stickler spoke up. "You can't trade lunches! It's against school rules! You can't trade lunches! You can't share food!"

"Nobody's asking to trade for *yours*," Daniel said, "so you don't need to care."

"I'm telling the lunch lady," Homer said.

"Sure thing, Homer," Nate told him.

By the time the lunch lady at the desk made her announcement, Daniel had Tyler's pizza, and my salami sandwich with spicy mustard was still with Nate.

"No sharing food," she said, hardly looking up from her phone. "School rules."

"Yeah," said Tyler, "school *rules*," and everybody laughed and the lunch lady probably thought we meant it. Homer just packed up his thermos and cleaned the cracker crumbs off his desk.

Sydney came up and tapped Nate's shoulder. "Did I hear somebody say they were trading a salami sandwich? I've got a chicken roll."

"A chicken roll?"

"Yeah," Sydney told Nate, showing him her plastic lunch container, "chicken in a tortilla."

"Is that like a burrito?"

"Maybe," she said. "It's cold. Does that count? And some of the ingredients are different."

"Yeah," Nate said. "I'll take it." He gave me a look.

I handed over my former salami sandwich on a roll with spicy mustard once again, but this time to Sydney. She peeked under the bun. "Is it buttered or anything?"

"Nope."

I was glad to give it to her. I'd rather have her eat my sandwich than Nate. Nate was happy about it too. He had a silly look on his face and I hated it so I told Sydney, "Enjoy your sandwich," and she smiled and said, "Good luck on the math test today," and Nate rolled his eyes.

I still ended up with Nate's bologna sandwich.

Nate took a couple of bites of Sydney's chicken tortilla. Two minutes later I was laughing at him when he called back to her, "There's no cheese!"

"Duh," I said, "she's allergic."

Unrolling the tortilla, he demanded, "What's *in* this?"

Sydney's face was red. I hated Nate for yelling at her. That's all I was thinking about. I knew the stuff Sydney's mom cooked and saw that the chicken tortilla was shredded chicken with white bean dip to hold it together instead of cheese. It was just bean spread and Nate was acting like it was some big deal, making Sydney's face all red as she ate my sandwich in the back of the room.

Nate stood up and stared at her. Everyone else was staring at her too. "Come on," I said, "stop picking on her. It's *bean dip.*"

Nate stood stretched like a rubber band, ready to go. "Shut up, Itch."

Sydney's head was down on her desk and her friends next to her were pulling her up and one of them was crying and the lunch lady asked if someone was choking and Maria booked it out of the room. Nate pointed at Homer. "You," he said, "right now. Where's your stuff?"

Nate had figured it out before I had. So had Homer. Sydney was having an allergic reaction. Anaphylactic shock. Her face was red and puffy and watery with tears and a runny nose and drool because her tongue or lips or both were swelling.

I don't even know how I got to the back of the room but the next thing I knew I was dragging Sydney out of her desk and laying her down on the floor, and Abby shoved stuff out of the way to make room for her and she held Sydney's hand and Sydney looked at me and I could tell she was scared. Her face didn't look like her face at all anymore. I was careful with her head on the hard, cold floor, and Nate was there too, and he was all snarl. "I'll punch you," he said, and I said without even thinking, "I'll punch you back," and Abby told us to shut up.

Looking at Homer, I told him to hurry up and do it. Give her the shot.

"Now," Nate said.

Homer clutched the zippered pack with his EpiPens. "Maria went to get the nurse?"

Nobody knew for sure. The lunch lady was on the phone with the office.

"We don't have to wait for the nurse," Nate said, grabbing for Homer's pack.

"Stop it. I can't do it."

"What do you mean, you can't do it? Stop being a wimp."

Everybody shouted at once. It was a lot of different sounds and words and voices but it all meant the same thing: Go. Do it. Now.

I'd wrapped my hand around Sydney's braid and Abby squeezed her hand. Sydney squeezed back. She didn't say anything. Her eyes were swollen shut. Abby had her other hand on Sydney's stomach and Abby's hand moved every time Sydney breathed, and that was all I wanted to pay attention to.

"One minute," Homer said. "I'll give the nurse one minute." He knelt down next to us.

I don't know if Homer was scared or not or if he was being Homer, the person who wasn't going to break any rules. What if one minute was too long to wait? Sydney always said, *Epis first, Epis fast.* "You wouldn't be hurting her," I told him.

He looked at me then. His face was as pale as a chicken's egg. "Unlike you."

I'd been so scared I hadn't even thought of that part yet. That I did this to her.

The nurse ran in. She had Sydney's EpiPens in her hands and she knelt on the floor and then boom, click. Just like Sydney had shown me with her trainer. She popped off the blue safety tab and stuck Sydney's outer thigh, right through her clothes. Blue to the sky, orange to the thigh. That's what Sydney had said when she'd shown me how her injectors worked.

One one thousand. Two one thousand. Three one thousand.

Outside, ambulance sirens wailed and it was the best sound in the world. I never thought a siren could sound like a good thing. When Mrs. Anderson skidded into the room everything was a mess. Kids huddled in the back of the classroom. Desks covered with uneaten lunches pushed everywhere, chairs knocked to the floor. Mrs. Anderson made all of us but Abby go out into the hallway, all the way out by the gym. Maria, crying with her hands over her face, escaped to the bathroom.

Nate's face was flushed the way it was after gym class. He couldn't hold still. He bounced on his toes. Swung his arms. He jabbed my shoulder. "This is your fault, Itch. What was in that sandwich of yours you were bragging about?"

"I wasn't bragging."

Nate and Daniel crowded close to me and no one else would look me in the eye. Not Lucas, who'd turned to face the wall, and not Tyler, who'd crossed his arms and looked like maybe he'd join in too, like if someone was going to start chanting *Fight, fight, fight*, it was going to be him.

Daniel started. "What was in your sandwich, Itch?"

They asked so many questions I couldn't have answered them even if I'd known what to say.

"Why would you do that?"

"Aren't you two friends or something?"

"Don't you know what she's allergic to, Itch?"

"Where was your famous air sandwich?"

"How come the day you don't have an air sandwich, you give it to Sydney?"

Nate still hadn't stopped moving. Even when he pointed at me he swung his arm a few times to fix his aim and his hand flexed. "I will punch you. I will punch you right now. I will clean your clock."

That's when I laughed in Nate's face. I laughed in his face right then because I was sick and sad and scared and it was one of those times when you just didn't know what you'd do, only that it would be wrong, and because I didn't know what was in my sandwich that hurt Sydney. I laughed because Nate's sandwich had been wrapped up funny and he'd said *clean your clock*, which is something I'd only ever heard my grandfather say. It's old-fashioned for beating somebody up, mostly the head.

"Go ahead." Maybe it would wipe out the image of Sydney, red and swollen, lying on the floor.

Nate sneered at me and shook his head as though my reaction was so wrong he could never punch me now.

I started to itch.

Homer said, "Don't."

"Don't what? Don't punch him?"

As long as the guys were talking to me he was practically invisible. He could have stayed invisible. "Don't itch."

"Yeah," Nate said, "don't itch, Itch."

"Aren't you making it worse?" Homer didn't mean Nate.

What did he know? I kept scratching the skin by my shirt collar. For another minute or so it would be a relief but then the beast would take over.

When Daniel told Homer, "You're a coward," I realized that wasn't true. Homer was brave. He stood up to Nate. He could have stayed invisible right now in the hallway while we all felt sick and mad and scared, but he didn't. Seeing Sydney like that probably was the scariest for him, because he knew. If it hadn't already happened to him, he knew it could. And now he tried to help me.

Tyler said, "You could have saved her."

Homer said, "The nurse was there. Sydney's going to the hospital."

"You missed your chance. You could have done something. You'd have been awesome."

Shaking his head, Homer said, "The nurse did it better. She did it right. I was just the backup." I knew Homer well enough that he'd had a million questions swirling through him as he'd held his meds and stared at Sydney on the floor. Homer was skinny. Sydney probably weighed more.

Maybe they had different dosages. Maybe there was something else I couldn't even come up with because I wasn't Homer.

I kept itching.

I said, "She's going to be okay." I couldn't imagine it any other way. Talking wasn't easy. Nate's bologna sandwich was stuck up in my throat. It felt totally indigestible. It felt like it would be there forever.

I said it again. "She's going to be okay." Nobody else said anything.

She had to be okay.

At the nurse's office I took my medicine. "I couldn't get ahold of your dad," the nurse told me. "Don't you have a backup emergency contact? That part of your form is incomplete. You should really have a backup."

"We don't know anyone here," I told her. "We moved from New York. State. That's where everybody is." When she gave me a look, I told her, "My family everybody."

"How about a friend's parent?"

I thought about Sydney's parents on the way to the ER. "No."

Dad and I hadn't managed to update my medications at school and all the forms and so I had to take the older medicine. It tasted a lot better but it didn't last as long and eventually conked me out. I hadn't taken my new medicine this morning the way I was supposed to. I'd thought it was overkill to take something every day for something that happened once in a while and might not even stop it. Maybe it wasn't. But being sleepy was a good thing. I'd sleep until my dad came to get me. The dark nurse's office with its green cots and paper sheets never looked so good. I'd stay there forever.

It turned out that the principal was looking for me and they still hadn't found my dad, and eventually I made the mistake of opening my eyes and the nurse decided to escort me back to class.

"I can't go back."

"Sure you can," she said.

"I'm not awake."

"Your hives are pretty much gone and the swelling's reduced."

What did it matter if I went back to class? Sydney was in the hospital. Because of me, Sydney couldn't breathe. Because of me, Sydney's heart pumped too slowly to move her blood the way it was supposed to. Because of me, Sydney might die.

As we walked together through the quiet hallway I was too sleepy to plan my escape. To think about running. Boom. Gone. Bye. Out the door. Just run somewhere.

Home. The farm. Straight to China. My brain and my legs weren't really working together and the idea and my commitment to it didn't really join up until it was too late and the nurse blocked me in by my classroom door.

"Don't you understand what happened in there?"

"I do," she said. "Everybody will be fine."

"Sydney?"

"Sydney will be okay. You will too."

She was lying about the second part. I just hoped she wasn't lying about the first.

All the rows were back in perfect order and everyone sat in their seats. Sydney wasn't there. The room was very quiet. Everybody looked at me. I looked at nobody. When I walked by Nate on the way to my desk he said, "Enjoy your sandwich."

Mrs. Anderson passed out the math tests. I couldn't believe it. How could she still expect us to do this? How could anyone concentrate? How could this be fair? But everyone else picked up their pencils and leaned forward and got to work. I felt the choke coming a mile away. I didn't even hope for good luck.

When I looked at the test I couldn't even think. I knew I was supposed to know this stuff—I thought I knew this stuff—but I didn't. My only hope was partial credit but then all I could think about was my dad and how he'd say that thanks to partial credit there were people in this country who were building bridges and they'd never even gotten one whole math problem right in their lives. Ever.

I flipped over the math test and looked out the window. Out in the distance I saw the dust cloud that ran along with a farmer's harvester. I put my head down on the desk and fell asleep.

CHAPTER 14

LOOK, I CAN tell you right now how part of this ends.

I never found a good food for lunch and I never loved peanut butter the way I used to, but maybe that's how it goes.

At lunch, Sydney sat with Abby and Maria full-time. Lucas drew a picture of me eating in the corner—my hands were fat and my sandwich was crying. When he showed it to me he didn't look mean about it. He might have been trying to be nice.

The cafeteria was finished in December, two weeks after the OSU-Michigan game. It turned out a cafeteria was just a cafeteria: once we were back it was so usual and ordinary it was as though we'd never been without it. It's not like anyone forgets how to eat in a cafeteria. Even though lunch hadn't been cooked in it for two and a half months, it still smelled like hot meat and steam.

Dad gave up. That's not how he said it, though. He said my school lunch was my problem to solve. He said it was a problem only a kid with plenty of food could have. Once the roof was back on and the cafeteria was open, he loaded up my school lunch account and I could pick whatever I wanted. Some of the food was good and some of it wasn't good and some of it was downright awful, but I ate it anyway. My mom was right about the cheeseburgers. They weren't bad at all. I kept an eye out for frog legs. Peanut butter was back but I didn't want it. That spring, I signed up for the track team.

But that's all what happened later on. That's all the easy stuff. This is what happened right after.

The day after Sydney's anaphylaxis, the whole class had to write essays on school rules and why they were important. And the whole class had quiet, indoor recess for a week. Daniel and Tyler also got a week of detentions. Nate and I had two days of in-school suspension and meetings with the principal—me with my dad and his wild-man beard, and Nate with his grandparents. In-school suspension was served in a little room with no windows off the back side of the gym and near the janitors' office, and even though we were in this dark, claustrophobic space we heard screaming gym-class kids and clanging from the janitors. The teacher was a man I'd never noticed before. His beard was as big as my dad's and he had yellow, chalky fingernails even though the blackboard in the room looked clean and

d-new. He gave us packets of work from Mrs. Ander-
and would let us talk, but only if we talked about fan-
tasy football. So I had nothing to say and Nate was happy.
Nate sat at the front of the room. I got the back corner. The
only other kids there were two fifth-graders who had gotten into a fight on the playground. I kind of thought that
maybe the school needed two separate rooms of in-school
suspension to keep the kids who hate each other apart, but
I learned later there were already two. One for everybody
sixth grade and below and one for everybody above. I kind
of felt like a pheasant in a pen with Brutus. I just kept my
head down.

The school nurse called and talked to my dad about the
itch and my dad put a pill out for me every morning next
to my OJ. He'd give me looks too, when he set it out for
me, and none of them were the same. Some meant that I
was irresponsible, that I should remember something this
important. Some meant that he felt sorry for me. Sometimes he rubbed my head, and his look then meant he was
doing dad stuff, like making me eat my vegetables. Some
were just about hurrying up and getting it done. Sometimes the itch happened anyway.

The first day we were out of in-school suspension, Nate
punched me. Boom. Just like he said he would.

We were out on the far side of the track behind the

school. At the center of the track's dirt oval was the football field. We weren't allowed on it. Cold metal bleachers rose up on one side of the field. It was far enough away from school that there was only time to get out there, run around the track four times, and then return once we were done. Mr. Mullins stayed out there with the last, slow kid, and as we each finished we headed back to the locker room on our own. The trek was a long diagonal across the empty soccer fields, the gym-class fields, and the edge of the parking lot.

Next week was Halloween, and I couldn't believe Mr. Mullins was dragging us outside for gym at the end of October. The cold and then warmth of the running and the rubbing of my clothes on my skin had me fighting the itch. I wanted to be quick and get it over with, and I'd never been that fast but then I took off and it was like I was on the bike, busting out, bursting through.

Mr. Mullins shouted to the kids behind me. "Slackers! Catch on up!"

I did my four turns and ran straight off the track, past the creaky bleachers, and out to the empty fields and back toward the gym.

Nate stood by the soccer goal. Waiting for me. I didn't realize he was waiting for me.

"Hey," I said, slowing down to a walk and breathing

hard. "Did you cut out?" Because there was no way he beat me here.

He punched me. Shot his hand out and punched my face. "Enjoy your sandwich." Then he punched my gut so hard I fell to the grass and then he was gone and I was alone.

My lungs squeezed. I tried a great big breath but it was just an empty shudder, then another, and then I got air, my heart thumping, my gut aching. The other kids caught up to me as I walked slowly back to the school, hunched over and with my hand at my eye. Homer and Tyler and Daniel and everybody else, talking football and Halloween costumes. They oozed around me and kept on going.

Mom wrote me a lot of emails saying she loved me. She called me up too, the night it happened. "Oh, Isaac," she said, and her voice sounded hollow and far away. "It was a terrible mistake," she told me after we were both quiet for a long time. "You're allowed to forgive yourself."

"What happened happened," I told her, "so I don't think it matters if it was a mistake or not."

"Have you talked to Sydney? Talk to Sydney. She'll feel better. You'll feel better. Would you like me to call her mother?"

It was sesame seeds. Not dairy or peanuts. Sesame seeds in the bun. Not on the bun, but *in* the bun, ground up, mixed in just like the flour, I guess. I read the label a few times to triple-check and quadruple-check. Sometimes things people are allergic to are bolded or listed in a special place, but not sesame seeds. So I didn't notice it right away.

Dad read it too. He gave me one of those dad hugs that's part hug, part lung-crushing squeeze, part backslap. "It was an accident," he said.

"It doesn't feel like an accident."

"You didn't mean to hurt her."

He didn't remind me that there are rules for a reason or anything like that and it was such a deep relief I think it made me cry more.

"Do you want to go see her in the hospital?"

I shook my head and threw out the buns.

I didn't see Sydney again until the day after my in-school suspension ended and Nate punched me, and then I made it all worse.

I'd only been out of class for two days, but right then the gym where we were eating felt big and unfamiliar and I didn't know where I should try to sit. So I just stood there. The gym was full of loud lunchtime kids. Mr. Mullins blasted on his whistle. We were supposed to sit on the bleachers but kids were still everywhere, coming in from their classes, bumping around me.

Daniel knocked into me. And then he was right up in my face, pressing his hands on his cheeks and mushing his face together.

"Look," he said, through fish lips, "look at my fat face." He kept sticking it closer to me.

Sydney showed up, yanking down one of Daniel's arms. "Stop it."

"I'm goofing."

"Stop picking on me," she told him.

"I was not."

He scowled and ran up to the back row of the bleachers. It was just me and Sydney. I hadn't talked her since that day. I didn't know how to do it. Everything felt like slow motion. My brain didn't work, and any words I had were stuck down someplace where I couldn't get to them. I'd never had to think about words with Sydney before. I'd never had to think about anything with Sydney before.

"What happened to you?"

I touched my eye. It hurt. It was ugly too.

"Did Nate do it?" She had her brown paper lunch bag crunched up in her fist, and I wondered what she had. I wondered what it was like to eat food again, after what I did to her. She was still waiting for an answer and I was still all knotted up and about to make everything worse.

Because this is what she said next. She said, "Why are you not even talking to me anymore, Itch?"

Itch. That's what she said. That's what she called me.

Then she was as gone as a fish in the ocean, lost in the moving crowd of lunchtime kids loose all over the gym. Mr. Mullins still blasted away on his whistle, and I left too, for the long and empty blue hallway far away from there.

CHAPTER 15

Mom: *Dad says you're not going trick/treating tonight.*

Me: *Because I am GROUNDED.*

Mom: *Did you dress up for school?*

Me: *No way.*

Mom: *There's a harvest moon tomorrow night.*

Me: *What's a harvest moon?*

Mom: *Full moon closest to the autumnal equinox.*

Me: *What's that?*

Mom: *The first day of fall! This year's harvest moon is later than most years. Be sure to look. If you look, you can't miss it.*

Me: *For scientific purposes?*

Mom: *Because it's amazing!*

Me: *Okay.*

Me: *Do they have Halloween in China?*

Me: *When are you coming home?*

On Beggars' Night, Dad came down into the basement between doorbell rings. "Sydney came by a little while ago."

I sat up on the bed. "She did?"

"Sure. Dressed like a zombie with a lot of red makeup dripping down her face."

"What did you give her? What are you giving out this year? She's got allergies. You can't just give her anything."

"Give me a little credit here."

"Mom's always got all kinds of stuff. Stickers for the little kids. She says everything's a choking hazard. And she has pretzels. Or boxes of raisins. Dad. Tell me you didn't give her a box of raisins."

That made him laugh. "It wasn't a box of raisins."

I'd been trick-or-treating with Sydney before. She collected her candy in a pillowcase like everybody else and then swapped it all out at home for candy her parents had that was stuff she could eat.

I flopped back on the bed. Itch. She'd never called me that before. "She probably made a mistake." I hoped that was what had happened with my name. It was bound to happen, right? A fish can't always swim upstream. All the same, though, I missed being me. "She probably didn't even know it was my house. You know. With a mask on and everything."

"Yeah," my dad said, patting my arm, "and because this town is so big and she's never been here before."

"And everybody knows our house," I said.

"Is that so?"

"We're the only one on the street without a Buckeye flag. Or an Ohio State welcome mat." I looked at the poster from Sydney. It was the only football thing in the house.

"So I've heard." He held up his hand. "Only from you. It's never come up with any other living soul."

"I meant that Sydney forgot it was our house." Because why would she ever come here again?

"Is something going on between the two of you?"

"Duh, Dad. I nearly killed her."

"Did she punch you? Is that how you got your black eye?"

"Nobody punched me, Dad. I ran into my locker."

He shook his head. "You and Sydney are too close to not get past this. Have you tried talking to her?"

Why are you not even talking to me anymore, Itch?

"Um, so she was a zombie?"

Dad looked at me for a while before answering. "Yeah. Fourth one of the night." He shook a small purple box of candy and handed it over to me. "There's more upstairs if you want some."

I wondered what she looked like. I wanted to ask something like, *Was she a brain-eating zombie or a cookie-eating zombie?* because Sydney would laugh at that.

Aside from fetching me on Saturdays, it was the first time Sydney had been back since the storm.

Since before.

When we sat in the basement with our helmets still on and in our muddy shoes and later Sydney said I'd saved her life.

You saved my life. You saved my life. You saved my life.

I didn't even think. I was past my dad, banging up the basement stairs, out the door and onto the sidewalk. *You saved my life.* Outside it was cold but not yet dark. Up ahead, at the end of the block, I caught sight of a group of three kids—I couldn't see much, just somebody in white, somebody with a red cape, and a third person wearing a pointy witch hat. Dad said there were a lot of zombies. Maybe it wasn't her. And maybe it wasn't a zombie. I wished she'd been a cookie. She'd be easier to find.

"Sydney! Sydney!"

Up ahead, the superhero and witch peeled away from the zombie. The zombie's face was covered in white and red makeup. "Sydney?"

Can zombies talk? What if all she said was zombie

talk? What if she looked at me and all she said was, "I'm going to eat your brain"?

We stood there a minute. Sydney the zombie stood patiently as though she expected me to say something. I hadn't thought that far. I'd only thought as far as busting out of the house.

Do you know what I said? When I had my chance, when I should have apologized or asked how she was doing, or maybe even just said hello, I said, "Trick or treat." Because I choked.

Somebody laughed. The zombie tilted her head. Her braid slid loose of its zombie rags. Without saying anything, she held out her partially full pillowcase, and I dropped in the cardboard box of candy I still held on to. It was crushed some from my fist. She stood like that for a little while, holding the pillowcase open. Next to her, her friends were restless. The superhero had a mask over her eyes. She shifted her weight back and forth. The witch swung her bag of loot over her shoulders. Her face was painted green, and she glared at me.

I didn't realize until later that Sydney was waiting for me to say something else. More. I was supposed to say something. Showing up wasn't enough.

So we just stood there until someone knocked shoulders down the row of girls and one of them said, "Let's go," and they turned away and went up the steps to Sydney's house.

They went inside. Dylan sat on the porch step. He wore his football helmet and a Buckeye jersey.

Dylan said, "That was weak."

"I know."

"Whatever you were trying to do."

I cleared my throat. "Apologize," I said. "I was trying to apologize."

"Weak," he repeated. Then he asked, "What candy did you give her?"

"Nerds."

"Eh. That makes it a little better." He was shoving candy into his mouth. "Mom said if I handled the kiddos I could eat everything I didn't give away, so I mostly gave away the stuff I don't like." He looked me over. He made me nervous. All he said, though, was, "Where's your costume? I can't give you candy without a costume." He held something out toward me. "You got to say trick or treat."

"I'm not trick-or-treating," I said. "I'm grounded."

"That's okay," he said. "Take some peanut butter cups. I got to move the nut stuff." He dropped some into my hand and I stuck them in my pocket where they'd get gross and melty and I wouldn't want to eat them anyway. "Mom's upset with her."

"What?"

"Yeah, because of the reaction thing."

"Your mom shouldn't be mad at her. She should be mad at me. It was my fault."

I guess I was loud because Dylan gave me a look through the face mask of his helmet.

"She's not supposed to share food. She can only eat her own food or she has to see an ingredients label. Like, a lot of store bread usually has dairy in it so it's always a problem. So forget the sesame seeds."

"It wasn't her fault. It was my fault." She knew it was my fault.

"She broke the rules."

"I broke the rules."

"Well, I guess you both broke the rules." Candy wrappers crinkled and Dylan asked, "So how are the birds?"

"Um, good." Why was he being nice to me? If Sydney were my sister, I wouldn't be nice to me.

"Are you down about the birds?" His mouth was full. "It's kind of a bummer when they start getting moved out. Not going to lie. But, you know, I didn't want to be a kid who didn't know a farm chicken and nuggets aren't the same thing. I mean, I know there are no pheasant nuggets, but you know what I mean."

"Are you still taking the job back in the spring?"

"Depends on baseball. Maybe I'll split it with you."

"Okay."

"They don't taste bad," Dylan said, surprising me. "Pheasants. Maybe Epple will make you some pheasant stew. He brought some by for us once. It wasn't bad at all."

"Did you know he can't really hear?"

"Sure," he said.

"I didn't know."

"Sorry if I forgot to mention it," he said. I thought it was a pretty major thing to forget. "Sometimes it's better if you write him a note if you have a question or something. Hey, do you want some more candy?"

"No. Thanks."

Heading home, it felt spooky like Halloween should, the way the wind moved the branches of the trees like they were hands scratching the night sky. The sky was just dark. No stars. No moon. Some little kids ran around me, plastic pumpkins banging against their legs. Ninjas and princesses and video-game characters and more superheroes.

Then this other thing came out of the darkness. It ran right toward me. Thinking about Nate and his punch, I flinched and dodged to the side, but the running thing did the same and crashed into me.

It was Bigfoot. A kid my size in a Bigfoot costume. A furry fabric shirt and some furry fabric draped over his head for hair and then some more for a beard, and a pair of brown gloves. White sneakers poked out of the bottom of some furry pants.

"Hey! Sorry!"

With the dark and the fur I couldn't see who was in the costume, but I recognized the voice right away.

"Homer? Jeez, man, you've got some unexpected skills."

That pulled him up short. "Itch?" He didn't sound happy to see me and he didn't think what I said about skills was a compliment. "What's that supposed to mean?"

"I mean, you're skinny and all but you're good at knocking people down."

Homer said, "Looks can be deceiving." Rocking back on his heels, he swung his candy bag as he pointed. "Is that your house?"

"Yeah." I waited for him to say something about how it wasn't decorated, not with Halloween stuff and not with Buckeye stuff, but he didn't say anything about it at all.

Instead, he asked, "Who are you? What are you supposed to be? Where's your costume?"

"I'm not really out. I'm grounded."

"What did you do?"

I hadn't even told the whole story to Sydney, but something made me tell Homer. "Skipped school."

"Oh," he said, "I don't blame you."

"Seriously?" I'd been hoping to shock him. I'd get a kick out of that. He'd wave his arms around and scold me and his eyes would bug out and maybe I'd forget how pathetic I'd been, trying to talk to Sydney.

He kind of shrugged. It was hard to tell, the way he was covered in a fur shirt. "Well, if you cut school and you're out here now violating your parole, you can go up the block with me."

Trick-or-treating was scheduled for two hours. It had been going on for a while, and now the streets were emptying out. I looked for Nate and Tyler and Daniel but only saw the same group of little kids who'd run past me right before Homer ran into me.

"Who are you out here with?" Was he out with the guys? Did they stay in town? They hadn't even asked me. They didn't know I was grounded, did they? They'd probably gone to the towns with the big neighborhoods and good sidewalks and miles and miles of candy.

Homer pointed up the street at the group of kids. He pushed the piece of furry stuff back off his forehead. "I thought I'd see more people out here. From school. Now that I know more people. Classmates. You know. Friends."

"Sydney was just out."

Homer squinted at me and I shrugged. "I saw her. With Abby and Maria." I left out all the rest.

"What about the guys?"

"They usually go somewhere else. To the town. To one of the rich neighborhoods."

"They didn't invite you?"

"Like I said, I'm grounded." I didn't point out that they didn't invite him either, but I guess he already knew that.

He scuffed his unfurry white sneaker across the sidewalk. "Do you think they'll always see us as new kids?"

I snorted. "You've got the bus and the party." Homer bled scarlet and gray. Heck, he *sneezed* scarlet and gray. I didn't have any awesome trick up my sleeve like the Buckeye Bus.

"I can't wait for the party. It will be different, after the party. You're coming, right? You haven't RSVP'ed yet." Homer crossed his furry arms. "That means you didn't *répondez s'il vous plaît*, to the invitation."

"I told you, I'm grounded. I can't come."

His mouth hung open. "Not even for this?"

"Sorry."

"But it's going to be great."

"Yeah."

The pack of kids started shouting and waving at us, and Homer waved back.

"Those are some kids from my youth group," he said,

"and some old homeschooler friends." *Homeschooler* sounded different when he said it.

"Homer, those are all little kids."

"Yeah, I'm kind of a group leader, if you can believe it. Hey, your dad! He actually gave out candy I can eat."

Homer pointed to my dad, standing on the porch. He didn't wear a costume either, just the roadkill on his face. "Your dad knew I was Bigfoot. And, man, I didn't know about his beard. It's like *he's* Bigfoot. Maybe we're related?" He laughed and I laughed too. "Actually," Homer said after a little while, "I'm the Ohio Grassman."

"What?"

"That's the Ohio Bigfoot. He's supposed to live out east. East in Ohio."

"No way. No way. There's a special Ohio Bigfoot?"

"Grassman. That's the name. For the Bigfoot in Ohio."

"That's a bad name. I mean, that's a really bad name. Why isn't it the Buckeye Bigfoot or something?"

We laughed and Homer said, "Tell me about it." Then he said, "I don't know. Maybe Grassman is some specific scientific classification. Like, Grassman, Sasquatch, Yeti."

I laughed some more, because that was classic Homer.

The kids up the street called out something. I couldn't tell what it was. It wasn't *Homer*. Waving, he shouted, "Coming!" Then he looked at me. "Come on!"

When I didn't move he yelled for the kids to wait up.

"You need a costume."

His group had crossed the street. They were opposite Sydney's house, which made the idea of going with him more appealing. It didn't mean we were a team. It meant I was lonely. And Homer, he seemed different out here. He wasn't Homer. He wasn't the same kid he was in school. He even moved differently. Like he wasn't thinking about it too hard. It was a lot easier to think of him as one of the guys or even a friend and not the kid who thought we should team up.

"Come on," he said, "come with us."

"I don't have a costume."

"You should have a costume. I mean, how much longer do we have Halloween for? In a couple years we'll be the big kids running around in lousy costumes and all the grown-ups will be giving us the stink eye."

I looked over at my own personal Bigfoot, still standing out on the front porch with a big bowl of candy. I stuck out my arms and shrugged. That was my *Can I go?* Dad gave me a thumbs-up.

"I've got an idea." Homer dug through his candy bag and eventually pulled out a pair of thick red mittens. "My mom packed them. In case it was cold. Like the Ohio Grassman has red mittens." He held them out for me but I didn't take them. "Come on. With these and your black eye you can be a boxer."

"Are you sure?"

"Well, look, it's no Ohio Grassman costume but it's not bad. And I'm in costume here so it's not like anybody will know you're with me. And, you know, trick-or-treating in a group isn't exactly a blood oath of friendship."

"I don't mean that. I mean everything else. I mean the sandwich swapping. And Sydney's reaction and all the rest."

Homer pushed the mittens at me. Inside they were warm and soft. "Get better," he said, "not bitter."

CHAPTER 16

I REPLAYED MY ENCOUNTER with Sydney on the sidewalk on Beggars' Night over and over. How she just stood waiting. How I didn't say anything. "Trick or treat" didn't count. It's too embarrassing to count. It was worse than saying nothing at all.

At school the next morning I wrote her a note. *Sorry.* I folded the page of notebook paper into triangles until it was as hard as a rock and held it hidden in my fist, thinking about how to give it to her.

All around me, kids were talking about trick-or-treating. How much candy they got. Their costumes. The good costumes they saw. The houses where people went all out with talking skeletons and fancy lights and spooky sounds echoing out of garages.

Somebody asked Lucas about his costume—an elaborate, homemade *Star Wars* costume—and when he was done talking about how he made it he said to Homer, "I saw you and Itch. That was a cool costume, Homer. You weren't a Wookiee, were you?"

"Nah," Homer answered. "Bigfoot."

Lucas nodded and started drawing in his notebook.

"Grassman." I said it under my breath. I'd been sitting slumped with my arms crossed, holding my note for Sydney against me, but when I saw that everybody had heard me I sat up straight. "Homer said he was the Ohio Grassman."

The guys did exactly what you think they'd do, and burst out into loud laughter.

"Tell me, Homer," Tyler said, "does the Grassman climb buildings? What's that called?"

"Schoolering," someone said, and then someone else said, "No, it's buildering."

"Right. Right. Self-explanatory."

Homer squinted up his eyes at me. "Itch was a boxer."

"Ha! Cool." Nate stuck out his fist, but since the last time I'd seen his fist he'd punched me, I didn't bump him the way he wanted. Nate knew exactly why too. He laughed. Then he pointed at my black eye. "I told Sydney I avenged her."

"What?"

"That's right. Since it was your fault."

"What did she say?" *Why are you not even talking to me anymore, Itch?* When did Nate tell her? What did she say?

How did she react? Was she glad? I wouldn't have thought she'd have been happy about Nate punching me, but I didn't know anymore. Not if she was calling me the same stupid thing everyone else called me. I could still hear her voice from that day in the gym. I couldn't decide how she sounded. Sad? Angry? I snuck a look at her across the room. *Trick or treat.* When I finally found some words that was all I'd had. The note's corners poked into the palm of my hand. *Sorry.* It wasn't very good, was it? And why would she even want to read my note? I mean, Nate's punch had said way more to her than that *Sorry* line and a tiny box of candy ever could. Right? Like the sign the football team had hung up by the bleachers: DEEDS, NOT WORDS.

Nate's face settled into something less proud of himself. "She said none of it was my business and that punching people was stupid. So when are you getting the birds? I got to know so I can be ready."

That's when Lucas showed us the picture he'd drawn, which was Nate riding a pheasant as if it were a horse. The pheasant looked more like a chicken. I didn't tell Lucas that. Lucas had drawn a word bubble for Nate: *Please!*

Nate looked at the picture and said, "Yeah, that. With a cherry on top?"

Mrs. Anderson called for eyes up front. I decided to pay attention to her and ignore Nate. She announced she was going to put us all back in our math study groups. Maybe we were supposed to get quieter then, but we only got louder. Mrs. Anderson held up a hand like a stop sign and stood there for a minute before she said, "You know, let's switch up the groups. I think we need this."

And then the class was all moaning about how we'd just had the test last week, which made us all think about Sydney, who knew it. She glued her eyes to her desk.

Mrs. Anderson put us in new study groups. Sydney's group was up at the front of the room by the door and I was in the opposite corner in the back of the room. Me, Tyler, and a girl I'd probably never ever spoken to, so that was good. Tyler leaned across and asked, "Are you getting Nate those birds soon?"

He wore a Toledo Mud Hens shirt, and I got some of that pig farm smell from him, probably from his boots. Tyler would be the first to tell you that it's not the pigs that smell, it's their poop, and that's what he told everybody, and he'd say that the stinky poop smell was the smell of money.

I shrugged. Tyler flipped open his math book. When I went to sharpen my pencil at the front of the room I detoured by Sydney. I put the folded-up note on her desk carefully, as if it wasn't just a piece of paper folded into a triangle. As if it might crack or break.

"Excuse me, Mr. Fitch? Have you lost your way back to your seat?"

Sydney didn't touch the note.

Kids snickered and I mumbled, "No," and when I got back to my desk I snapped off my pencil's new sharp point and Sydney took her braid and drew it across her eyes and held it there until Mrs. Anderson tapped her shoulder. Even then, she arranged her braid in a funny way so it sat on the side of her face. She curled it around her ear to make it stay in place.

Nobody gave her a second look or gave her any trouble for sitting there like some sideways *Star Wars* character.

My eyes burned. Sitting at my desk with my math book open in front of me, I thought of a hundred different, other, better things I could have written to her besides only *Sorry*.

Daniel leaned over and flicked the paper triangle away and off Sydney's desk as if it were a game of paper football.

I wanted the itch. I wanted it to grow inside me and simmer on my skin and boil out and *go*. I could fall to the floor and itch just the way everybody always said I did— like a dog on a rug, my leg thumping because I didn't have a tail, and whine that dog whine that's somewhere between happy and suffering. I'd go and go until I was as puffy as a dead gassy fish just waiting to explode.

Maybe Mrs. Anderson could use it as a math lesson

easy enough for me to get. "Look, class, here is Mr. Fitch. Seventh-eighths of him is covered in hives. How much of him remains?"

But that's not the right equation. It's backward. That seven-eighths that's hives, that's all me.

Even Sydney saw it now. How I was all itch.

I rubbed my neck. Scratched my hands. Sawed my arms against my rib cage. Pressed my forearms down hard on the desk and scraped them down across the desk's edge, over and over again. And it started. I was glad for it. Relieved, maybe. That's what that itch was. Relief. Giving in. Knowing that this was it so I might as well just do what I wanted.

Off to the side someone snuffed. Huffed. Shifted in their seat. I could tell it was Homer. I could hear his big wet eyes rolling.

I didn't raise my swollen red hand to ask to go to the nurse's office. When I scraped my chair back it tipped and I caught it before it fell but I ended up knocking everything off the desk, and my number-two pencil sounded musical as it rolled onto the floor.

I grabbed my stuff and waved. *Yep, here I go, I'm Itch, I've got hives and swelling again, excuse me, I'll just be going to the nurse's office.*

Once there, I took a dose of my new medication, the

way I'm supposed to after the itch starts. The nurse let me stay there until we were sure it worked, and then a little longer until it was lunchtime. "Don't think I'll let you do this every day," she said.

And then Mrs. Anderson showed up. "Mr. Fitch. Why don't you come join me for lunch?"

The rest of the class herded past her, probably on their way to the art room again. Nate said he heard when the cafeteria finally opened it was going to serve steaks. Homer said, "Who cares about steaks? I want a tree-nut-free, peanut-free table. Will there be one of those?"

Sydney walked next to Homer. "Sure," she said. "Anybody can sit there, as long as their lunch is okay. I just want to eat in a big room again. In a room where we can talk loudly. Don't you wish—" She stopped talking when she saw me.

And do you know what I wanted? I wanted her to say *Trick or treat* to me. It would be mean. But it might also be funny. I'd say *Trick or treat* back to her, and then I'd say I was sorry and maybe something else I didn't even know I wanted to say. I wouldn't even care if she called me Itch.

Back in the classroom Mrs. Anderson sat at her desk and I sat in a desk from the front row she'd pulled over next to hers.

"You know, Mr. Fitch," she told me, peeling back the

plastic cover on a steaming microwave lunch that smelled really good, "you can eat lunch in here anytime. I'm usually working on things, and my door is open. You don't need an invitation."

"Oh," I said.

"If you don't really like where you're eating lunch that day, or the company." She looked right at me then, waited for me to say something, and then dropped the plastic film in the trash by her desk.

"Okay," I said. "Thanks."

She stirred her lunch—it looked like ravioli but it didn't have anything red with it—and I started on my sandwich (ham). She told me she'd heard my mom was in China on business. Her brother had lived in China for a year. "What city is she in?"

"Suzhou." I said it carefully the way Mom had me practice it as we drove her to the airport. She said we should pronounce it correctly. Even if we didn't get it exactly right, she said we should take the time to try. "It's near Shanghai." I'd checked a map. I'd even looked up her hotel. The website didn't say if it had a waffle maker or not.

"Very cool."

"It's been two months. My dad's growing a beard. It's wild." I didn't tell her all the rest of it. It was a lot of things, but it wasn't cool.

"Sounds like your mother has an interesting job." Long pause. "Is she the one who helped you with your math?"

"Sometimes. Sydney used to help me too. But, also, I didn't used to need help."

"Ah." That's when she laid my test faceup next to my lunch. Except for my name and my number ten next to it, there wasn't a mark on it. I'd written nothing else and she hadn't written anything on it either.

"I think you can do better than this."

It was funny. "Yeah. I sure hope so. I mean, it wouldn't be too hard, right?"

"Can you take the test again next week?" Even though she got down to business, she was smiling too. "Let's say sometime during lunch? Next Tuesday?"

"You're letting me take the test again?"

"I sure am."

"Can you do that?"

"You bet," she said. "I'm the teacher. I can give you a retest."

I'd flipped the test over. I hadn't even doodled on it. I didn't even fake it. I didn't even try. I'd stared out the window, watching the dust trail of a giant farm machine harvesting. Instead of solving equations, I watched a soybean field go from green to dirt.

"It seems unfair. I mean, everybody was pretty upset. I'd think everybody did lousy."

"What's fair isn't always obvious. It doesn't mean that everything is always the same for everyone." She leaned back in her chair so she could watch me better. "I graded the test on a curve. I can't curve a zero."

"Oh."

She smiled then, as though my reluctance really surprised her. "Are you trying to talk me out of it?"

"No! I mean—"

"One of your best friends had just been taken to the hospital. And weren't you having an episode yourself?"

When she called Sydney one of my best friends, something let loose inside me. Calling Sydney one of my best friends wasn't exactly right. Not anymore.

"Everybody knows it was my fault. It's not like I deserve a break."

"What's wrong with me giving you a do-over? There's nothing wrong with a second chance. Can you imagine? What if instead of a season your team just played one game? Or if the winner of the game was the team that scored first? And then that's it—one point?"

She was smiling and I knew she thought she was giving me something awesome and I shouldn't have felt so deflated about it, but I did. There wasn't much I could say about it, though. "Okay."

"Good. I also want to give you fair warning. I've contacted your father." She held up her hand to stop whatever I might have said. "You know it's school policy. Now, finish your lunch and find a pencil. We've got some reviewing to do."

Dad was home from work early that day. He was waiting for me in the kitchen. "It's good to see you," he said. "How was school?"

"Are you going to make me quit the pheasant farm?"

Dad walked into the dining room and set down the bowl of pretzels he was carrying. "How about we take this one step at a time." He pointed to a chair. "Let's get started. Get out your math book."

He'd cleared off the dining room table. The only things on it were his special mechanical pencils. Mom always had some cloth going down the middle of the table and some candlesticks with brand-new candles we never lit because they were a fire and air-quality hazard. Usually she had some decorations out. Maybe some little wooden pumpkins if it was Halloween, or a glass turkey for Thanksgiving. Dad had moved the summer decorations, a bouquet of brightly colored fake flowers, that had been out since Mom left.

"Tell me about this retest."

"Mrs. Anderson is letting me take the test again. She's giving me a second chance." Saying it out loud was different than just thinking about it.

"That's good. It's good of your teacher to do this for you."

"I put my head on my desk and fell asleep the first time. I didn't even try."

Dad arranged his fancy mechanical pencils next to my open math book. He rubbed his beard. "It was a bad day."

"It was the worst."

"Did you find Sydney? On Halloween?"

I said no. Not really. I could tell Dad wanted to follow up on that, so I asked, "Did you know your beard would grow like that?"

"Not quite like this. I'd never gone longer than a week without shaving."

"Are you going to keep it?"

He rubbed his cheek through his beard. "Probably not."

"Good. It's weird. You look like someone else. Do you feel like someone else?"

"No," he said. "I forget about it until I look in the mirror. Then I'm surprised."

"Really? I don't believe you. You itch it all the time."

"What can I say? It itches."

That made me laugh. "Dad," I said, "you don't know itching," and he laughed too.

"No, kid, I guess I don't."

And maybe it shouldn't have been fun or funny, but it was. Dad shook his head and finished laughing. "Are you going to tell me how you got that black eye?"

"I already told you," I said, "I ran into my locker. The corner part. At the top. They're short. The lockers."

He didn't believe me. After a while he said, "Let's get started. We'll go slow. Let me know if I go too fast—"

"Or make those frustrated noises if I don't catch on."

"What frustrated noises?"

"Those big sighs."

"Big sighs?"

"Yeah," I said, "those big sighs when you think I'm missing something obvious. I'm just going to tell you right now, Dad, nothing about any of this is obvious to me."

"Okay," he said, "got it." He handed me one of his special pencils. "If I do that you go ahead and break one of the pencil points." That sounds silly but for my dad it's serious. He's had those pencils since college. He doesn't like to share them, not even with Mom, and once I lost one of the metal eraser caps. He was not happy.

I looked at the book and the opened, unmarked pages of my notebook, the cleaned-off tabletop, and Dad. I don't know. I didn't want to quit the pheasant farm. And maybe it wouldn't be so bad. Maybe this would be the thing we'd figure out how to do together while Mom was gone.

CHAPTER 17

M R. EPPLE DIDN'T care about my black eye. When he'd seen it all he said was, "No trouble. Not if you work here," and then he turned and walked away and that's all there was to say about it. He didn't wait for me to agree or disagree or explain anything about it.

It was November. Except for the new fields of winter wheat, as green as golf courses, the farmland had turned brown and bare. Mr. Epple had started emptying out some of the pens. Every Monday when I came there were fewer and fewer birds. The front two pens were completely empty. I scrubbed the empty feed and water containers and thought about Sydney, Mrs. Anderson, multiplying fractions, making things divide into pieces and then making them more again.

The farm was the only place I'd been able to follow any of my itching rules. No itching, check. No itching in front of witnesses, check. So I was covered on my third rule. No itching at the farm. All I'd ever had was an itchy feeling.

Which was funny, because no itching at the farm was the least important of all the rules. Mr. Epple wouldn't care if I swelled up like something out of a horror movie or a gross internet video clip. I'd just do my stuff and he'd leave me alone. The birds wouldn't care either. Not as long as I had their food. Maybe they'd think I was showing off. Maybe they'd think I was puffing up and I was the biggest, baddest bird in the pen.

I liked how Mr. Epple left me alone to do what I was supposed to do. I was glad he wasn't that interested in me. It felt good. Right then, it was the only thing about my life that was easy.

Even if I'd decided I was going to get Nate a pheasant egg.

Because an egg was better than nothing.

And I'd been thinking about second chances.

An egg would be easier to take than a bird, even though a bird was what Nate wanted. An egg would be easier to transport than a pheasant even if it would be harder to steal from the barn because Mr. Epple always counted the eggs. Not like the pheasants, which I counted.

Slip the egg into a pocket, keep it warm against my body, and walk my bike out to Nate's storage unit.

When I imagined it, I tucked the egg inside my work gloves and put my work gloves inside the deep pocket of my cargo pants and I walked along the road steady and easy. When I imagined it, it seemed important. Taking care of something. Because an unbroken egg meant something, it meant something after I'd broken everything.

When I give the egg to Nate, he holds it in his hands as if it's beautiful and important to him too, and he says, "You did it, man. You did it. I didn't think you would. You're okay after all." Sometimes, when I imagine him holding the egg carefully, he says he knows it was an accident. "I know that. Everybody knows that. You didn't mean to hurt her."

Or he'd give the egg back. He'd give the egg back and say, "I don't need an egg, man. I don't want your dumb peace offering." He'd say, "What's this for? I don't need this. You stupid Michigan fan."

If I got a chick, it would die. Mr. Epple kept everything just so. The temperature. How much space each animal had. How much food and water, and even the location of the feed containers. When a chick hatched or was moved from one box to another, he picked up each small bird and dipped its beak in the water so it would know what water was and where to find it. Heat lamps hung low and glowed red over each box. Mr. Epple checked the thermometers all the time and moved the heat lamps up or down.

And taking a pheasant? Impossible. How would I do

that? I could slip away with an egg. But pheasants were real, squawking things that would run away as soon as they hit open ground.

But I could get Nate an egg. I could show everybody who voted for me to get Nate a pheasant. I wouldn't be the kid who nearly killed Sydney. I wouldn't be the kid who used to be from somewhere else. I wouldn't be the kid who wasn't a Buckeye. I wouldn't be the kid who itched. Next time I passed Sydney a note, she'd read it.

Mr. Epple, off doing his own work, waved. Waving back, I stared at the red brooder barn, thinking about stealing an egg. Planning it out. I'd have to do it soon. He didn't have any eggs or chicks or birds after January when pheasant season ended. Dad hadn't made me quit yet, and he hadn't given me a minimum test score I'd have to beat if I wanted to keep working. All he ever said was *We'll see.* And I had to steal an egg soon before I remembered what was right and what was wrong. While I thought it was a good idea.

I imagined giving the egg to Sydney. She cups it in her hands. The egg is warm. Sydney knows what's inside. She looks at it in wonder. She knows exactly what it means. "Thank you," she says, "thank you, Isaac."

I opened my eyes and saw the pens and heard the

pheasants in the brush and remembered how I'd blown it on Halloween and how she wouldn't even read my sorry *Sorry* note. Dad and Mom both said I should talk to her. Call her up on the phone. Knock on her door. They didn't know how I'd tried and how I'd just made it all worse. Stealing a pheasant egg for Nate in comparison seemed like a piece of cake.

Once I started thinking about stealing as a second chance, it got easier and easier.

Get into the barn. Slide my hand, palm down, over the warm egg. Get the egg into my pocket.

Coasting by the Storage-U after on my bike, I heard the *thwap-thwap* of a ball hitting the metal doors. The road rises right before the gravel driveway. It slowed me down. *Thwap. Thwap.* The light was on in the office. The top of Nate's grandma's hair showed through the window. *Thwap. Thwap.* Nate was playing slow. He was bored.

Except for class, I'd avoided him since the punch. What else could I do? I hid out at lunchtime, took my sandwich and slipped away to a wide spot in the hallway near the busted cafeteria or went to the spot by the band room where Sydney and I had studied.

Nate's basketball rolled out under the partially closed door of the storage unit. He stood at the opening and stooped down, watching the ball roll away down the gravel drive, and then he spotted me.

"Nate!" My bike bumped over the gravel as I hollered. "Hey, Nate!" Tipping to one side to plant my foot, I kicked the ball back toward him.

The door rattled all the way up. Nate scooped up the ball and stood there in the dark space, holding the ball in front of him like he was going to shoot me a hard pass. "Yeah?"

There was something I had to know. "Are you going to scramble it?"

"What?"

"The egg—are you going to scramble it?"

He gave me a look. I knew what it meant. *Too stupid for words.*

"If I get you a pheasant egg, are you going to scramble it?" I didn't tell him he couldn't scramble it. There was a bird inside. Curled and wet and ugly.

His face blanked. "Shut up," he said. "I want a *bird.*"

"I can't get you a bird. If you want a bird you have to find another way." It was impossible. Ridiculous. I'd seen Mr. Epple do it, one afternoon when one of the birds made a break for it, and I knew it wasn't anything I could do.

That time, the rooster hadn't gone far. It ran around the yard and then stood outside the pen looking at all the birds on the inside. Mr. Epple picked up the bird with his crooked fingers, tucked the wings in gently even though the bird wanted to flap, and dodged the bird's spurs. He shouted something about his jacket, so I grabbed it off a post where he'd hung it and followed him into the pen. When he let the bird go, it flapped its wings and flew into the brush.

We spent the rest of the afternoon wiring up some netting over the top of the pen where the bird had flown out. Mr. Epple told me the holes had to be big enough to let any snow fall through but small enough to keep the pheasants in and foxes and whatever else out.

I asked Mr. Epple, "What was the jacket for?" By then I'd figured out that in order to hear or understand me he had to see my face and my mouth, so I made sure to look him dead-on.

"Wrap it up." He swirled a finger as if it explained everything. "Wrap it up if it had a mind of its own."

Nate said, "I'm not going to scramble it. Why would I do that? I'm not going to do that. That's insulting. I just want the bird. You know, put it in a box and shine a light on it and have the bird. The pheasant. I don't want an egg. An egg's too risky."

"I can't do a bird." After Mr. Epple had recaptured the

bird I'd gone online and read about handling pheasants, and I didn't think it was something I'd be able to do. "A bird's impossible. And not a chick either. It'll die two steps from the barn."

"Come on, man. Why are you making this so hard? I thought we were friends."

That made me sit back on my bike. "You punched me."

"Yeah," he said, "I was mad."

"You shouldn't punch people."

Nate shrugged. "Sorry." He said it like it was easy. I wondered if he really meant it.

I kept seeing Sydney, how she'd looked on the classroom floor. How she didn't even look at me anymore. How I didn't talk to her anymore.

"Can you believe Homer?" Nate asked. "I still can't believe it. He could have saved her. For real this time, not like in gym class. He had the medicine right in his hands."

"The nurse came." Right after Sydney, Homer must have been the most scared person in the classroom, even more scared than I was.

Nate just shook his head like he was disgusted with everything, and we were quiet for a minute, probably both of us feeling sick, remembering what it was like while we waited for the nurse to run in and give Sydney her shot.

Nate said, "I'd take good care of it, the bird."

I started to pedal away.

Nate hollered after me. "So you're getting me one?"

Like Mr. Epple, I just waved.

Right past the Storage-U is the only downhill on my route. It's not much. I hit it as fast as I could. In town, my bike kept going. I rode past my house and on toward Sydney's. I thought about what my dad said, that we were too close to not be friends.

Maybe she'd be out on the porch, reading or playing cards or doing her homework. If Daniel hadn't flicked the note away, would Sydney have read it? What would she think? I'd bike by now, and maybe she'd say hi. Maybe I'd look surprised to see her. I'd say hi and then I'd say I was sorry. She'd say something like, *I know you're sorry, tell me something new, why don't you,* and it would be a joke and it wouldn't be awkward for very long. She might not even call me Itch. She's only about a block away. My house is in the middle of my block, and then across the street she's three houses up. If I'm fast, we're practically neighbors.

Maybe I'd tell her about my plan. About getting Nate an egg. *That's awesome,* maybe she'd say. Maybe she'd ask why. I'd tell her I was doing something for my friend, for all of my friends. For her. I'd ask her if she wanted an egg. I'd tell her, *If you want an egg, I'll get you an egg, I promise.*

And if Sydney was going to hate me forever—egg or no egg—I wanted to know. I wouldn't blame her. The bike bumped over a sewer grate and my stomach flipped up and it gave me a little wave of sickness but I felt hopeful too.

As soon as I got close to her house, I saw her two brothers in their football jackets sitting on the porch rail. They were laughing and maybe arm-wrestling and they were pretty loud. Dylan stood up when he saw me and yelled, "How are the birds?" I gave him a thumbs-up and turned home.

Since what happened with Sydney happened, Mom decided we had to video chat twice a week. She used her phone. I'd only see a piece of her face at a time, and there were a lot of lags. I'd say hello and wait and then I'd think I should say something and I'd start to tell her about my bike or something and then she'd pop right into the middle of my sentence and wave and say, "Hi, sweetie!"

I wished I could talk to her about how I'd decided to steal a pheasant egg for Nate, because I knew she'd have a lot of good ideas about how to safely carry something so fragile.

She asked, "Are you putting one-third of your money from the farm into your savings account like we agreed?"

I tried to joke with her. "We said a quarter. I only had to save twenty-five percent, not thirty."

She jostled her phone around and so I said, "I'm going to buy a new bike," and she came in right in the middle of my sentence with, "See! You are getting your fractions! Are you ready for your retest?"

It always went like that.

I told her I couldn't decide which kind of bike to get, a sleek and aerodynamic road bike with skinny wheels and low handlebars, or a mountain bike with sweet suspension and fat, knobby tires for riding along the muddy riverbank. I left out the part about the riverbank. She came in the middle of one of my sentences to tell me she saw a lot of bike riders.

Would riding my bike at the river even be the same without Sydney? Even if we were still friends, would she be too busy with Abby and Maria?

"I hardly see any helmets." Mom sounded as sad as when she found out about what had happened to Sydney. Mom finally held the phone as far away as she could and then I could see her whole face. "So many cyclists," she said, "but hardly any helmets. Promise me you're wearing yours?"

"You know I am. Will you be back before—"

"Good. Good."

"—Thanksgiving?"

"You bet," she said. "Good luck on your test. Love you, buddy."

CHAPTER 18

THE SATURDAY BEFORE my makeup test, Ohio State lost to Michigan State. The Michigan State Spartans—the other school from Michigan—are not the Buckeyes' archrivals. It was the second-to-last game of the season. I'd watched half the games alone, grounded. Dad never watched. Next week was the big rivalry game and Homer's party that I couldn't go to and then Mom would be home and then it would be Thanksgiving. The Michigan State game was played in the cold, dark, and rain. On TV, the game was the center of the world. Bright colors. Lights. The flicks of rain on the coaches' faces glittered. The stadium was filled. "Record crowd here tonight at the Shoe," one of the announcers said. Beyond the lit-up stadium, the whole world was darkness.

"That's what they always say," Dad said. "It's always a record crowd."

I didn't answer. He sat next to me on the couch and watched the end of the game. He'd never done that before.

The fans cheered and waved. Some wore rain ponchos and some guys didn't wear much more than body paint.

Ohio State lost on a last-second field goal. Three points.

It was like all the air had been let out of the balloon. That's what the announcers said, and they were right. *Whoosh.* All the people in the stands who'd been moving the whole game, bouncing up and down and waving, dropped their arms. The game on the field was over and the Buckeyes lost and so no one in scarlet was jumping around and the band didn't move or play and the only thing that happened was that the coaches ripped off their headsets. I could picture what it was like at Sydney's. People stuck standing—everybody on their feet to watch the final play, and then when it had gone wrong they were frozen in disbelief. Her dad groaning. Her brothers so upset they couldn't even get out a real sentence. Sydney's hands over her mouth.

The Michigan State players moved. They jumped up and down and bumped off each other and pushed their faces in the camera. There weren't as many of them, though, as all those Buckeye fans, so they seemed small and lonely, even if they were triumphant.

Dad slapped his hand down on my knee. "Good game."

I gave him a look of disbelief. "What?"

"Close. Suspenseful. There's going to be a lot of

bellyaching about it at work tomorrow. All those armchair quarterbacks."

"They lost. They haven't lost in…" I couldn't remember when they'd lost. At least not in the regular season.

"You can't win them all. You know that. It would be boring too."

"Dad. There's nothing boring about winning. Winning is winning. It's all about winning. That's the object of the game." How did he not get that?

"Just think how exciting it will be if they beat the other Michigan—"

"The *other* Michigan? How can you not even keep them straight?"

He waved me off. "This will make it way more exciting if they beat the University of Michigan next week."

"No way." Last season when I watched all the games at Sydney's house, the Buckeyes rolled over everybody. It was awesome. It was awesome to sit down on Saturday and know that your team practically had superpowers.

"This way, when they win, it'll be even more exciting. Pulling together. Digging deep. Finding out what they're really made of. All those things the commentators always say."

He's told me practically the same stuff about my

schoolwork before. About dividing fractions. He told me that once I'd learned something hard I wouldn't just have learned how to do that thing but also how my brain worked. I told him I liked it better when I just *got* it. I'd asked him, *Wouldn't you rather I aced it the first time?* He'd said it was a learning opportunity.

"Last year a guy broke his leg during the game and they still won," I said.

"Sometimes, when you're a kid, it's hard to believe that your team can lose."

"Who was your team?" That made me wonder. "What's even your *sport*?" Dad laughed. "A long time ago," he said, "I was a Boston Red Sox fan."

"So?"

He laughed some more. "Well, when I was kid they were famous for not winning a World Series in ages."

"Yeah, well, that was a long time ago."

Monday, the game was the only story at school. Michigan State 17, Ohio State 14.

"It was a close game," Daniel said.

"Good teams win close games." That was Tyler. He wore a Boston Red Sox T-shirt, but I didn't say anything to him about it.

"No way," Nate said, "The score was close. The game wasn't. We didn't play worth nothing." He shot a finger at Daniel. "Nothing."

"A close score is a close score. How can you argue with that?"

Homer said, "I don't know what the coaches were thinking. There were lots of inefficient and uncreative plays. They should have been much more aggressive about running the ball."

Nate crossed his arms hard enough to hear. "No kidding. That's what I said two minutes ago."

Homer said, "Well, that was kind of just a cliché."

"A what?"

"And it was actually a little unspecific."

"Are you kidding me?" Nate threw his hands up into the air.

Daniel leaned across the group and whispered loudly, like always. "Guys. My neighbors? They've got a kid who goes to school in Michigan. They have a Michigan flag hanging up in their garage."

"Darn straight it's in their garage."

"State or University of?"

"Does it matter?"

Nate sat all hunched and scowled up. "*Uncreative*," he muttered. He didn't care about Buckeye traitors sixty miles from the state line. He cared about Homer and Homer's vocabulary words.

Then like magic, Homer changed the whole conversation. "You guys ready to turn out for the Bucks at the party next Saturday?"

"You know it!"

"*O-H, I-O!*"

He was still Homeschool Homer, but he got to pull the Buckeyes out of his back pocket and just like that Nate and everybody were happy again.

Grabbing my lunch, I left them all to talk about the Buckeyes and went to the quiet and empty dead-end hallway where Sydney and I had studied. The test was tomorrow. Maybe I'd do okay. I'd have to do okay. If I stayed messed up in math there was no way Mom or Dad would let me keep working at the farm. It would have to be all math all the time.

Homer had left all that Buckeye talk and followed me. He hung back like he was stalking me, carrying his lunch box and his math book and notebook, and I spotted him peering around the corner. By the time he caught up with me I was already sitting on the floor, looking at my math book and eating an apple.

Homer said, "I heard you had a retest."

"That's personal information if I do."

"Do you want to study?"

I took another bite of apple before I asked, "Did you follow me?"

Homer shrugged. "Do you need any help? Because I'll help you. I'm not as good as Sydney, but I'm pretty good. I got a ninety-eight on the test. And that was just because of a careless error. It was hard to concentrate."

If I'd felt like talking with him, I'd have asked if that was his curved or uncurved grade. "I studied with my dad."

"Oh. Okay." He stood there funny, his elbows kicked up as he held on to his school things and his lunch, and like he'd stopped in the middle of a step. "Are you sure you can't come to my party? I mean, your dad let you go trick-or-treating."

The thing was, I hadn't even asked my dad. He might let me go but I wasn't sure I wanted to anymore. But I told Homer the truth, which was that my mom had already said no a bunch of times.

Then I asked what had been bugging me since he'd shown up. "Why aren't you with the guys? I mean, your big Buckeye Bus party is Saturday. You should be living it up. You can't do any wrong right now. You just lead the whole class in the *O-H* cheer."

He shrugged again. He said, "You know, Nate did okay. On the test. I think he got another B."

Why was he telling me this? Was he telling me that even *Nate* was smarter than me? And *that grade*, that grade had been the curved one, right?

"Do you think it works?"

"Studying?" I couldn't believe Homer would ask me that.

Shaking his head, he thumped his math book against the side of his head and he grinned, but it was an embarrassed kind of grin. "Osmosis. Do you think it works?" When I didn't answer right away, he added, "Remember how Nate said he studied? By sleeping with his head on his math book?"

Homer was weird but he usually made sense. "No," I said, "I don't think osmosis works for math." I made a face too. Like he was ridiculous. Because he was. Even if osmosis probably made about as much sense as a good-luck charm.

He said, "I kind of hope it does."

"Um," I said, and he just stood there in the hallway, still looking like he was hinged like a robot, and I thought about how different he was on Halloween when we ran up and down the streets, trick-or-treating. So this is what I did next. I thumped my math book to the side of my head too. Itch and Homer in a dead-end hallway, holding books against their heads. It was funny stupid but we didn't laugh very much.

By then I'd figured out that he wasn't really talking about math.

"Maybe it works," I said. I wanted it to be true. Osmosis. Right? Figuring out how to fit in just by showing up, just by being there, by living here. Wasn't that what I'd been doing for three years?

Then because it was awkward with him standing there, I asked him if he was going to sit down. I wanted to be alone. I didn't say that, though.

Homer shook his head. "I believe I'll go join Mrs. Anderson. She said I could eat with her anytime."

I lowered my math book. "You aren't eating with the class?"

"No."

"Why not?" Everybody was psyched about his party. "You're good now."

He took the book away from his head. "It's hard to tell."

I thought about saying he was fine, but he was right. It was hard to tell.

Then he said, "Be sure to get a good night's sleep before your test. It's really critical for your information retention."

That night Dad and I went over the study sheet again and he had some problems he found online and we baked a frozen round grocery-store pizza and I went to bed a little

bit early. Dad let me borrow one of his mechanical pencils.
I took the retest during lunch.

Mom: *How do you think your retest went?*

Me: *???? Maybe ok.*

Me: *The big game is tomorrow. And the party I can't go to.*

Mom: *Remember how empty it was at the mall? Are you and Dad going to go again?*

Me: *No way. Dad says you're coming back Monday.*

Mom: *Yes! See you Monday night at the airport!!!*

CHAPTER 19

THE MORNING OF the big game against That Team Up North, Dad woke me up early. At first I thought he was going to tell me I could go to Homer's party, and I wondered what would happen when I told him I didn't want to go anymore. Or maybe Mrs. Anderson had called him about my test grade. He'd only wake me up if it was good. He wasn't mean like that, to wake me on Saturday morning to tell me I'd flunked.

But that wasn't why he woke me. He had to go in to work.

"Today?"

"Yeah, today," he said. "The world doesn't stop just because it's Saturday."

"I mean because of the game, Dad."

He told me to take my face out of my pillow because he couldn't understand me.

"Dad, it's game day. It's *the* game day."

"The machines don't know that." Sometimes Dad had to go in on Saturdays to reprogram them. "You're still not going to that football party," he told me as he headed back up the basement stairs.

It had snowed overnight. We didn't get as much snow here as I was used to in New York, though we still got plenty. Usually it was the wind that made it a big deal. Wind whipped the snow across the roads and the snow looked like waves of white in fields, or like a carved, frozen ocean. The snow that morning was different. Big, heavy, wet snow. The kind that's for snowmen and is hard to shovel and when it warms up it slides off roofs in avalanches.

The snow changed everything.

Standing on the bed to look between the slats of the blinds on the basement window, I knew what I was going to do. I knew today was the day and I knew how I was going to do it.

I know it was only weather, but right then it felt like a miracle. And I know my dad having to go in to work was only work, but that felt like a miracle too. As if this one time everything was going to go my way. I was going to the farm. Mr. Epple needed me. He'd told me once how he lost half his birds one year when heavy snow made the pens collapse.

I'd get Nate his egg. Or eggs.

Egg, hand, glove, pocket, go. Egg, hand, glove, pocket, go, gone.

Upstairs in my regular bedroom, I dressed the way Mom would tell me to. Long johns and extra shirts too, and two pairs of socks, including one of Dad's really good pair of special wool socks, the kind that aren't scratchy.

I took my medicine just like I was supposed to and stowed the extra in my pocket.

And then I was gone. Out the door. Grabbed a ratty old towel from the garage for extra egg insulation and my bike off the front porch. Backpack on. Helmet on. It was tight, over my black, full-face ski mask. My helmet had a flashing light on the back. My bike had lights on the front and the back, and reflectors on the wheels.

The flying football flags hanging on the houses were bright red marks against a world of snow.

The roads were messy and thick with slush as the snow melted. Sometimes the bike rocked out from under me. Sometimes a foot slipped off the pedal. I was cold and hot at the same time—my clothes were wet but I was sweating.

I couldn't go fast. Pedaling through soup. I tried walking my bike because maybe that would be faster but it wasn't, and all it did for me was get my legs even wetter.

When a car drove down the street, waves of slush

fanned out behind it like a wake from a boat. The drivers all stared at me. Sydney's car went by. I could see her in the backseat, her hair in a ballet bun because it was Saturday morning and she had a class before the game.

If the roads had been good I could have caught up with the car. In town with the speed limit and stop signs at the corners I could always catch up, if I pushed. But not in this stuff. At the stop sign, Sydney's mom turned left to drive to the town with dance classes. I went right. The press of the slush was loud and my ears were covered, but I thought I heard Sydney shout out the window as the car drove away. Maybe *Go Bucks.* Maybe *Beat Michigan.* Maybe. Maybe it was, "Good luck!" Even if that wasn't it, it carried me a little farther down the road.

My hands ached from clutching the handlebars and my lungs were about to burn out of me by the time I came up to the Storage-U. It was the most beautiful thing I'd ever seen in my whole life. Long rows of cinder blocks with red metal doors and a mix of old roof, new roof, and blue tarps.

It wasn't hard to find an empty storage unit. Nate's. The door wasn't shut all the way. Snow had drifted in. Though it was out of the wind, it wasn't very warm. I left my ski mask on. With all the sweat, my watery eyes, and my runny nose, it was probably frozen to my face anyway.

Nate's unit wasn't an empty dodgeball cage anymore.

A folding lawn chair sat open in the corner. Underneath it were a couple of empty sports drink bottles and some candy bar wrappers. Knowing him, it was probably a special raccoon trap. I pushed the door up higher so I could get enough daylight into the corners to be sure a family of skunks wasn't hiding out. Off to the side were a couple of desk lamps and an old and broken grandma's-house-looking chair that someone had probably left behind.

Then I spotted an unplugged space heater. Its cord was long and orange, and I knew that meant it plugged in somewhere outside and it wasn't long before I found it, an outside outlet covered with small outlet doors.

It was the best thing ever. The best thing I'd ever found in my whole life. A hundred-dollar bill at the side of the road couldn't have beat it. I sat in the rickety old lawn chair in my long underwear, the space heater blowing on me and drying my jeans I'd draped over the old chair's arm.

Nate also had a collection of empty soup cans. Every single one of them was clam chowder. There were a lot of them. All chowder. Everybody knew that if you worked at the soup plant you got free cases of soup. It was only one flavor, though. Maybe you'd get twenty-four cans, and maybe that seems awesome, until you realize it's all clam chowder. Or pea soup. A case of pea soup would be worse. Nate had stacked the empty cans into a pyramid.

For the first time, it felt like I was trespassing.

That's when I noticed it. By the desk lamps. A rough wooden box. Inside were some straw and sawdust and two empty bowls. Nate was waiting for a bird, just like he said. And he really was counting on me.

CHAPTER 20

*W*HEN I FINALLY made it to the farm Mr. Epple came up to me and thumped my shoulder. He laughed out loud. Happy.

We got to work. We each stood on a ladder and knocked off the snow covering the tops of the pens with brooms. It was hard work. My arms burned and my legs, already tired, shook from holding steady on the ladder. Inside the pens, the birds ran from one spot to another as daylight finally broke in.

I wondered what it was like, at the game, at the Horseshoe. It would be a sea of scarlet and gray. That's what people said when the stadium was packed (like it always was) and everyone was wearing their colors. And it would be loud. Loud all the time and then louder still during an exciting play.

Or what it was like at Homer's party. Would I have finally been able to say something to Sydney? Maybe we'd just sit next to each other and cheer together and that would be enough, just being together like the way it used to be. And if I were there, would I still be planning on stealing an egg for Nate? Or would everything be good?

We found four dead pheasants under some snow. Suffocated, Mr. Epple told me. "Not bad," he said.

When we were done Mr. Epple waved me into the brooder barn. I stomped the snow off my boots and slipped through the crack of the open doorway and then closed the door behind me. Light came in under the door and through a couple of high windows, but the inside of the barn was nothing but darkness and the red and eerie glow of the heat lamps. Musical cheeps filled the space like strange background noise.

It would be easy. Grab an egg, wrap it up, ride away. Except that wasn't my plan anymore. The miracle of the snow. Nate's storage unit. I wasn't taking an egg.

A TV played in the back of the barn. It was an old tube TV—a small black cube—with a blurry picture. Mr. Epple dragged over two solid white plastic chairs and pointed at them and I walked past all those easy eggs.

We sat in the barn in our coats and watched the game. We ate microwave noodles and crackers. The picture was lousy and the players looked small and fuzzy, not bright and big the way they looked on a regular television. It smelled like sawdust and birds. A space heater blew at our feet.

The sound was off. The Best Damn Band in the Land, Ohio State's marching band, played, moving soundlessly across the thick, square screen. It sounded as though all those shiny brass instruments only played bird noises. At the start of the third quarter, Mr. Epple turned up the volume and laughed a rusty laugh and smacked my shoulder and shook his head.

"So," he said after such a long while that his gruff voice startled me, "who won?" He pointed at the faded bruise under my eye.

I turned to look at him square. "Not me."

"That the end of it?"

"Maybe," I said. "Maybe not."

"That so." He pointed to his own face, his flattened nose and the unrolled scrolls of his ears. "Ugly mug," he said. He cleared his throat but when he spoke again his voice sounded exactly the same. "Fair fight?"

"No. But I deserved it."

He nodded. Then I told him I knew how to fix it. I said it out loud. But he'd looked away from me by then, so it was as though I'd only told myself.

The Buckeyes scored and the screen was filled with red rolling waves of cheering fans and players leaping in celebration, followed by a flash of the band playing. Mr. Epple smiled and shot a fist in the air, and when he watched the replay he did the same thing all over again.

The Buckeyes were driving toward the goal line. That's what the announcers said. My heart pounded, as if I cared about the game. Every time it beat it felt like a fist inside my chest.

By the time the game was over, the Buckeyes had won and the world was filled with fog.

I waved goodbye to Mr. Epple and acted like I was expecting a ride and waited until he went into his house. I couldn't even see him in the fog. I only knew he went inside because of the sound of his back door opening and closing.

I pulled on my ski mask. I looked like a bad guy on the news.

What time was it? Would I get itchy? How long would my medicine last? Would I need the extra pill? I went back to the pens. Those birds knew me, even if I was unsure of things, in the dark and in the fog. They were used to me. When I opened the gate a few walked over and crowded my feet, ready to follow me to the food and water. Most stayed put. They don't know anything about danger. Most of the hens were tucked down tight in the snow.

They didn't know danger, and they didn't know freedom

either. I left the door open. I figured I wouldn't be able to mess with the doors and the birds at the same time. But those birds, they didn't go anywhere. The way out wasn't obvious—two chain link doors covered with netting, with a turn between them—but the birds weren't even curious.

My pinky finger got hot and swollen, the way it sometimes did. *Itch here, itch here, itch me.*

Those birds, they came right to me. They had a few weeks to go before they got their full color. They were some of the last birds of the season. Then there would be no work until maybe April, when it would probably be Dylan's job again.

I dropped the towel on the closest bird. Clutched the edges in my hands and ducked down to wrap it, held its wings in. Not too tight. Not too hard. Didn't want to break anything.

I forgot about the legs. I forgot to hold the legs. I forgot to hold the bird upside down. That's what I'd read to do. Hold the bird upside down with a finger between the hocks. Hocks are like ankles. I'd looked it up.

I had a rooster. His whole body beat. I don't know if it was his heart with fear or the wings I held down. I hadn't wrapped him all up, and he stuck my leg with a spur. Not too deep. I had on jeans and long johns. It hurt, though. Sharp and fast. He stabbed again. I tried to get the towel over his feet, to get him upside down, and those spurs stuck my work gloves and my exposed wrist. I yelled and it hurt so much my eyes smarted and there was that feeling when it hurts all through your body. It was too dark to see blood, but I could feel my wrist bleeding, the opening of my glove sliding against it. How much blood was there? Was there an artery there?

"Come on, come on. Time to go, Not Brutus."

I held that bird upside down and all wrong. Wrapped up. My arms around it. Its feet covered but against my chest, not in my hands. The doors banged behind me.

I should have tried a hen first so I could practice on a bird without spurs, and I should have brought my backpack in with me. Why hadn't I brought it in with me?

Hands full of angry bird, I kicked the backpack open. I tried to shove it in. Head down. Wrapped in a beach towel. I thought I'd be able do better than that, but right then all I wanted was to get it contained.

Then click, flash.

The motion-sensor light on the barn flicked on. One of those pure white and blinding lights that makes every-thing look like the moon. I dropped the bird.

Except it didn't go down. I let go of the bird and it shot straight up, wings flapping hard. A few tail feathers fell off. It flew up vertically. It was beautiful and unlike any bird I'd ever seen, glowing in the white light and the haze of the fog, its colorful feathers shimmering. And then it was gone. It probably hadn't gone far but I didn't know. In the light, I saw the thin trickle of dried blood on my wrist and you'd think it would have been a bigger relief, that I wouldn't bleed to death.

When the light went off, I went back in, smarter, and grabbed a hen.

The fog made the whole world, everything—my icy bike and the bird, a quiet, warm slug of weight in my backpack— seem unreal. Lonely. It wasn't like I could exactly call my dad. Maybe I could try later after the drop-off. Under my chin strap and inside my mask, I itched.

I rode slow past the farm and past its wide driveway and wide gravel shoulder. Out to where the road was nothing but a white line to follow on my right and beyond it the big drainage ditch. And that's where I was—soggy with the melting snow, but not as foul as last time—when the Buckeye Bus rolled up.

CHAPTER 21

FIRST, THERE WAS only light. Headlights. Hazy and mysterious in the fog. Like what you'd imagine a spaceship to be if it had landed right there in the road.

I wanted it to be a spaceship. It seemed possible. Everything since the storm had been weird. Different. It would be so easy if that creepy light shining through the fog was an alien spaceship come to take me away.

But it was the Buckeye Bus.

An old-style short bus, it had a long nose and was painted a darker gray than the surrounding fog. Up over its grill and hood was a thick red stripe, edged with two thinner white stripes. Scarlet and gray. OHIO STATE was painted in block letters on the front between the headlights.

Taking off my helmet and ski mask, I stood at the foggy side of the road, my hands on my cold handlebars, that cold cooking through me, bird strapped to my back, as the door creaked opened.

"Hey, kid, need a ride?"

Inside the bus was dark and quiet. A party bus without the party. A postgame show buzzed on the radio. I didn't see any passengers. I didn't hear anyone singing "Hang on, Sloopy," which is something Ohio State football fans do. I didn't see Homer or Sydney or Nate or anybody. The bus clanked and something inside it clunked in a way maybe it shouldn't.

"Kid? Kid, need a ride?"

A ghost of a face appeared in the doorway. "Itch, it's me."

"Homer." Bus fumes filled my mouth.

"Yeah." He didn't sound very happy. "You don't live here," he said, squinting out into the darkness. "It's the bird farm."

"Pheasant."

"Pheasant farm." He looked at my bike. "Come on, we'll give you a ride."

I hauled my bike up the steps and into the bus, pushing it down the aisle until it ran into all the junk at the back. It wasn't like a regular bus inside. Two long benches ran along each side, under the windows, and the bus was crammed with gear. A grill. Bags of charcoal. A propane tank. Folded-up red tents and lawn chairs. Homer. And Sydney.

That fist feeling in my chest was back. Punch. Punch. Punch.

"Hi," Sydney said.

Punch. "Hi." Punch punch. Punch.

She sat across from Homer, her arm over a barrel of a cooler parents fill with orange drink for soccer games.

I was thinking about telling her I was sorry, just simple, just *Sorry*, like the note, because that might be all I could manage, when the bus jerked forward and the interior lights went off. The coolers on the floor slid forward and then, after the bus lurched, fell back. Everything smelled like propane and charcoal and bratwurst and barbecue and, at the same time, like the outdoors.

Homer's dad hollered. "Find a seat!"

I sat next to Homer because it was the first open spot.

"Where you headed?"

I gave Homer's dad the name of the roads that intersected by the Storage-U. "Okay," he said. "We're dropping kids off."

"Right," Homer added. "Getting the full Buckeye Bus experience. We just dropped off Tyler and Abby. Sydney was last." He paused. "But now there's you."

Homer's dad called back that Sydney was still the last stop.

She said, "Cool."

I sat stiff and straight. I couldn't lean back. I had to brace my feet on the floor and my elbows on my knees so I wouldn't crush the pheasant. The bird was quiet. *Please, bird, stay quiet. And don't move. But be alive.*

Nobody had much to say to anybody. Sydney looked out toward the dark window. Homer looked at me. I looked at Homer's dad's feet. We stayed like that until the bus lurched again and I lost my hold and fell back and the bird got her feet into me, right through my backpack and coat. "Ow!"

"What's wrong with you?"

The bird was still moving. I turned to face Homer so he couldn't see my backpack but I didn't have much hope I could keep things hidden for long. Homer wasn't the type of person who wouldn't notice that my backpack was alive. Trying to distract him, I said the first thing I could come up with. "How was the game?"

"What?"

"Um, the game? How was it?" He didn't answer, so I said, "You know, the only game that counts?"

Homer looked at Sydney. "How did he not watch the game? Who doesn't watch the game?"

"I meant," I said, "how was the game because of the party and the big screen and all that." I knew what it meant to him. "I *saw* the game." Most of it.

"Is that so? What was the score? What was the best play? Who was the MVP?"

"It's not like I rooted for Michigan, okay?"

"Hey!" his dad called from the driver's seat. "We don't say that word on this bus!"

"I was with the pheasants." I looked at Sydney. She wasn't ignoring me, exactly, but she was mostly looking out the window. "We had to knock the snow off the pens or the pens would collapse and kill the pheasants."

"Great," Homer said. "Now everybody can make money by killing them later?"

"I did it for Mr. Epple." Which was part true and also part of the biggest lie I'd ever told.

Sydney asked, "The birds would die under the snow?"

She still wasn't looking at me but out the window, and I could only see half her face.

"Right." And just like how everything else was all mixed up, when Sydney finally spoke to me after all this time, it was both wonderful and awful because she was only talking to me because we were stuck on the bus together. She thought I'd helped the birds and Mr. Epple. She didn't know what I'd really done. She didn't know what was in my backpack. "If the pens collapsed," I explained, "the birds would suffocate."

The bus shook and chugged and bounced me and Homer up and down on the hard bench, and I believed Homer when he'd said something to Nate about it not being up for the trip to Columbus.

Mostly, though, I was thinking about keeping the bird alive and keeping it hidden. Because how stupid would that be? To steal it for Nate, lose one while I was at it, and then have this one suffocate because I was just happy that it wasn't making noise and was scared stiff?

Homer's dad braked hard for a stop sign. It's a country stop sign at a four-way stop and it has a flashing red light so drivers can see it far away while they're going fast on flat, straight roads, and so drivers can see it in the fog. When I jumped up so I wouldn't crush the bird, Homer jumped up too.

"Hey! Knock it off!" I twisted away, and the hen gave up being a scared lump. Even though the bird didn't have room, she tried to fly. The noise she made was all wings.

"Whoa," Sydney said. "Your backpack is alive."

Homer lunged for the zipper.

"Don't open it, Homer," I told him. "Don't open it. Don't open it."

"Homer! Don't open it!"

"My name's not Homer!"

"But—his backpack really is alive!"

Homer ripped the zipper and the bird burst out and up, hit the ceiling, and then landed, stunned, on the cooler next to Sydney.

Sydney yelped and ducked and then held out her hand. "It pooped on me!"

Homer said, "That's not a pheasant! It's a big pigeon!"

I yelled back. "It's female!"

Sydney shushed us. "You don't want Homer's dad to hear us." She still held her hand cupped and away from her. "Are there any paper towels or anything back here?"

Homer shoved some party napkins at her while he scowled at the bird. "My dad is going to kill us. And that may or may not be hyperbole."

"What?" Sydney made faces of disgust as she wiped her hand.

"An exaggeration." Homer stared at the bird. The bird stared back. I didn't bother to tell Homer that any terrified bird will win any staring contest with a human, a female pheasant in particular. Even on the rattling and clanking Buckeye Bus.

"So gross."

Homer told her, "It's supposed to be good luck. When a bird poops on you."

"I doubt it."

"I guess, maybe, because what are the odds? You know, of it actually landing on you."

"Maybe if you're outside. Not closed up together on a bus. Because then I think the odds are very, very good that the bird poop will land on you."

We all looked at the bird and Homer asked, "Is it dangerous?"

"It's a hen."

"That doesn't answer my question."

"Don't worry about it," I said.

Sydney asked, "Can't you put it back in your backpack?"

"I'm pretty sure Homer destroyed the zipper. So I could put it in but I don't think it would stay there."

"She's glad to be out," Homer said.

Sydney said to Homer, "Yeah, but are *you* glad she's out?"

"Look, guys. Even if the zipper works, I don't think I could get it back in. It was hard enough the first time." I didn't tell them about the male pheasant, his feathers gleaming in the light before he disappeared into the fog and the dark.

"I can't believe you really did it," Sydney said, looking at me straight-on for the first time in ages. "You stole a bird for Nate."

"How can you not believe it? You guys voted for it."

That's when Homer said, "Stole, nothing, Sydney. He saved this bird's life."

"Not if he's going to give it to Nate," said Sydney.

I told them, "I think Nate will do right by it."

"Really?"

"Really." I thought about telling them about what I'd seen in Nate's storage unit, but it seemed personal. Sydney asked, "What if it flies up to the front? And if you can't get it into your backpack, how will you get it off the bus?"

Before I could tell her I'd wrap it up in a towel, Homer said, "I can't believe you're saving this bird. That's pretty cool."

I thumped back down on the bench. My bike fell against me. "Homer. It's not cool." Of all the weird things Homer had ever said, this was the weirdest. "I'm a thief."

"You saved the bird."

Sydney snorted. "Only if the bus ride doesn't kill it." The bird had hardly moved since it had landed on the cooler. "Or if it's not dead already."

It hit me then. I was trying to do what Nate wanted. I was trying to fix everything. But I was also doing the most horrible thing I had ever done on purpose in my whole life. It was against the law. I was a thief and a liar, and I'd been a thief and a liar to Mr. Epple. And now Homer thought I was doing something good?

"Great," Homer said, but he sounded sad and he didn't really mean great, not in the heavy, flat way he said it. "This is even better than my party. You're saving this bird's life *and* you got it for Nate. Right, Syd?"

"Homer, your party was amazing and you know it."

"I didn't exactly plan this. I didn't ask for a ride. And

just so you know, I was trying to help you out with Nate. Okay? When you spilled your tomato soup and Nate was about to explode, that's when I started trading sandwiches. Okay? I was helping both of you out."

Sydney gasped. I think it was Sydney. I still couldn't see her face.

"And it's not just for Nate. The bird. I mean, sure, he's the one who started it, but it's for all of you. You guys voted. It was unanimous."

"You abstained. It wasn't unanimous."

"It's to show you all that I'm not a bad guy. I didn't mean to hurt anyone. Sydney." I looked over at her. She stared at her feet. "You, Sydney. It was just a new sandwich. The roll. And we all started swapping, and then—" I stopped there because we all knew what had happened next.

Out of breath as though I'd been biking and yelling at the same time, I slumped back onto the bench. "Okay?"

Homer didn't answer, just moved his arms and legs around like he was thinking about folding everything up but didn't know how to do it. After a while he said, "Nate was the one who technically traded with her."

"I shouldn't have traded," Sydney said. "I know better."

Homer said, "Don't blame yourself."

Sydney said, "I need to protect myself. I can't eat anything if I don't for sure know the ingredients."

"It stinks," I said, and Homer said, "Get better, not bitter."

We were quiet for a little while. A bag of charcoal in the back rattled.

Sydney asked, "What are you going to do with it? The pheasant."

"Drop it off at Nate's storage unit." She looked like maybe that wasn't such a great idea so I said, "He's got it all set up. He's got a box for it and some sawdust and stuff and some food bowls." I couldn't remember if he had food in the bowls. Probably not. I wondered if pheasants could eat soup, since it looked like Nate could get a lot.

"Will it be okay there?" That was from Homer.

"Sure," I said. "It lives just fine outside."

Sydney said, "My cousins turned an old shed into a chicken coop. Isn't this about the same thing?"

"It'll be dark," I said.

"Maybe you should stay with it," Homer said, "just for the night."

Before I could tell Homer no way, Sydney said it instead. "Nobody's going to sleep at the storage unit, Homer. Not even you."

Homer sighed. Maybe he'd really been thinking about it. Probably. If he thought that me stealing a pheasant was awesome, I could only imagine what he'd think about camping out with it in Nate's storage unit.

"Here's what we could do," I said. "We'll grab some twigs and stuff to make it better for her."

"And we've got water," Sydney said. "We'll fill her water bowl from one of the bottles."

"Okay." Homer still didn't seem convinced. "I'll call Nate. He should know tonight, don't you think?" He looked at me when he said it. As if he was worried about stealing my glory.

Because I knew there wasn't any glory to steal, I told him, "Good idea."

He smiled then. "Great."

"Good."

Homer said, "This is a good thing you're doing, Itch."

When I went to itch my neck, both Homer and Sydney shouted at me. "Stop! Don't!"

"What?"

"Don't itch it," Sydney said. "It looks like a hive."

Homer peered at my neck. "Confirmed. It's a hive."

"So what if I itch it? I'm Itch."

Homer said, "You can't finish this if you're red and puffy and stuff."

"Sure I can."

"Didn't you take your medicine?" That was Doctor Homer.

"This morning."

"Does it help if you don't itch? Or is it impossible not to itch?"

"Itching makes it worse? Right?" Sydney asked.

"Yes."

"Yes to which one?"

"All of them." I took my second pill out of my zipped pocket and opened up its sealed blister pack and chewed it. It tasted awful, the same as always.

We were closer to town now and there were more lights, hazy haloes in the fog. Lights over garages. Lit-up houses still filled with Buckeye parties. If it wasn't for the fog, I bet we'd be able to see the big-screen TVs shining out at us. The bus chugged and hissed as it slowed down.

Sydney said, "You better put that bird away."

I laughed at that. She made it sound like it was a normal thing to do. Put away a pheasant.

Now that the bus had stopped moving, the bird decided to start. It stood up and flapped out its wings and made that *drum-drum-drum* sound. Sydney bolted over to our side of the bus. "Seriously! Do something. And do it before Homer's dad finds it."

We'd come to a full stop in the drive of the Storage-U. Homer's dad stuck his head back. He looked like Homer, only older and inflated. "This isn't a house. It's the storage place."

"It's where he's going, Dad! Wait a sec. I'll help him with his bike."

"I dropped every kid off at their house and watched them go in the front door. I'm not leaving anyone at a storage unit in the dark."

"He's got a thing to do." It was the most regular thing I'd ever heard Homer say. His dad must have felt the same way too.

"'A thing to do'? I don't even know what that means."

Sydney and I looked at each other. She tilted her head at the bird. I shrugged and reached into my backpack for the towel.

Homer told his dad, "Itch has to make a delivery."

Homer's dad shook his head and took a deep breath and then looked at Sydney and me and then back at Homer. "I'd like you to start making sense right now."

Homer pointed at me. "Itch is making a delivery to a storage unit here."

"What's itch?"

"He's Itch!" Since Homer was already pointing at me, he stuck his finger into my shoulder. "This is Itch!"

"Excuse me?"

"That's his name."

"That's no one's name."

"That's what we call him."

Homer's dad looked at me. "What's your name, son?" Then he held up his hand. "Hold on. Don't answer." He looked at Homer. "You tell me his name."

There was a long pause. I started to smile. I don't know why. Because it was funny? Because there was a pheasant on the bus and maybe Homer's dad hadn't even noticed it yet? Because Homer was getting in trouble? Because Homer was going to have to use my real name?

Finally Homer said, "It's Isaac."

"Isaac what?"

"Isaac Fitch."

"Thank you. Now. Isaac. I'm not just going to leave you here. You can call your parents if you like, and Sydney should call hers, since we're running late."

Homer said, "His parents are in China."

Homer's dad looked at me again. "Right. Fitch, I know your mom." What he said next iced up my gut. "I know how she'd want this done right."

Just then the bird shot up again, its wings flapping. I didn't remember it being so big. It was loud and had nowhere to go.

I yelled *I got it, I got it*, though I didn't. Homer's dad swore. Homer yelled out something about hollow bones, and Sydney said we should get off the bus. They all ducked. I held the towel. The bird thwacked around. Its wings brushed the windows, the ceiling.

"Just hold still."

I meant every living thing on the bus. I wasn't just wishing for the bird to hold still. When it did, I wrapped it in the towel and tucked it up under my arm as gentle as I could. Slid my hands around the legs at the hocks. Turned it upside down. Kept it tucked in like a ball on its way to the end zone. *Don't crush it, don't crush it.*

Open the door, open the door, open the door. I forgot to talk out loud.

Homer yelled, "Open the door, Dad!" Then he told me one more wrong thing. "Wow, Itch, you're really good at that," he said. "You look like you know exactly what you're doing."

CHAPTER 22

*D*O YOU EVER think sleep is kind of like amnesia?

After the bus dropped me off I showered and then didn't feel like going down two flights of stairs to the basement futon. So I slept upstairs in my real bed. Regular old twin mattress. Regular old comforter. Regular old walls and windows.

Waking up after sleeping hard, it was just morning in my old bedroom. All that was in my mind was a big sleepy blankness: white bedroom walls, white snow outside. Amnesia. Maybe there's a good kind. You don't remember the wrong things you've done. It's an eraser. You can start all over again.

Looking at my four plain walls instead of the basement walls, it was as though the tornado had never roared through town. Like maybe all of it had never happened. Sydney eating my sandwich. The pheasant that got loose and the pheasant I stole. The fog and the Buckeye Bus. Homer. Keeping the bird cornered in the storage unit while Homer and Sydney searched the snow for branches to make the place more bird-friendly. Homer's dad grumbling at us until Homer told him it was for a school project. Maybe Mom's been here all along. Yesterday, we went to the mall. Maybe I ate a triangular slice of mall pizza and a giant waffle ice cream cone, and the food court was so empty it echoed.

Thinking like that worked until I moved. My whole body was sore. My arms ached. It hurt to move my legs. And I saw the cuts on my hands from the pheasants. When I got home last night I'd scrubbed them and then loaded up with antiseptic cream. Would they get infected? A bird probably carried all sorts of germs. Then again, I'd been working with the birds since August without any problem. Mr. Epple never seemed sick or anything. The scratch on my leg wasn't bad at all. A red spot. The pheasant had made a hole clear through my jeans and long johns.

Then Mr. Epple showed up and knocked on the front door early Sunday morning while I was still in bed and Dad was drinking coffee and checking Mom's flights online. She was coming home Monday night. Tomorrow night. Her flights were booked. Shanghai to Toronto to Detroit, which was about two hours away.

Dad was glad to see him and shook his hand. It was a good thing he wasn't home last night when the Buckeye

Bus dropped me off. Dad must have thought Mr. Epple had picked me up yesterday too, because I hadn't heard anything about me and my bike and bad roads and fog and watermelon brains.

"Trouble," Mr. Epple said, loud enough for me to hear up from my bedroom.

Dad said, "Sure. I'll get Isaac."

I threw on yesterday's dirty long johns and shirts and jeans and covered my hands with work gloves. Dad made me gulp down some OJ and my pill and sent me with a granola bar in my coat pocket.

The drive out in Mr. Epple's truck was short. Yesterday, on my bike, the ride had felt like a triumph. Me and the snow and the fog and the pheasants and finally getting the pheasant hen safely shuttered in Nate's storage unit. But not now. Whatever reason Mr. Epple needed me on Sunday morning wasn't good and it was because of what I'd done yesterday after the game.

He didn't speak to me until we got to the farm. I sat quietly in the truck and sweated, listening to the engine and the whir of blasting heat.

The landscape looked new again in the snow. Like it had when I'd first driven out with Mom all the way from New York and it was all unfamiliar. Once we'd dropped south by Erie, Pennsylvania, our drive had been west, west,

west. We'd gone past cities and factories and the big lake and then it was country, farmland, green earth, and end-less, open land and sky.

We drove by the pheasant farm too, that first time. We didn't know what it was. I'd pressed my face to the window, looking to see what it was inside the pens, but I hadn't been able to see much then. It had only been June, so now I know that any pheasants Mr. Epple might have had would be young and hard to spot in the brush.

Mr. Epple parked his truck off the side of the road before the farm. "Quiet," he said, and when he got out he didn't even close the truck's door. I left mine partially open too.

"There's eleven missing," he said, as we slogged through the wet and muddy grass at the side of the road. At the farm, he gave me a bucket of feed and pointed me in one direction and he grabbed another bucket and headed in another. There was already a trail of feed in the leftover snow leading to the first door of the pen. That's where I found my first missing pheasant. A bright rooster, pecking his way back. He was easy. I just opened the doors, secured them behind me, and left out some more feed.

Then I checked the pen and the two doors again. Because that was why I was here. Because I hadn't secured the pen last night and eleven birds had escaped.

No. Nine. Nine birds had escaped. I'd stolen two.

Then I thought about the pheasant that had shot up in the bright security lights and how beautiful it was. Was it free? Was it out there? Was it some other animal's prey? Would we find ten birds? Maybe we'd find ten pheasants— the nine who had escaped the pen, and the one who had escaped me—and Mr. Epple would shrug the last one away, and then he'd never know, I'd never have to tell.

I'd done things all wrong. I could have paid Mr. Epple for the birds. I could have asked and maybe he would have said yes, or I could have sent Nate to him. There were a lot of things I could have tried, and this one was just a thousand ways stupid. Nate had started talking about stealing the birds and I'd spent so much time thinking about eggs that it all got jammed in my brain and I never tried to come up with any other, better way.

Mr. Epple was different than the other grown-ups I knew. He let me be. And though it was hard to see it at first, he was nice. He'd made me microwave noodles and we'd watched the game. I liked being out here, alone and not alone. I liked the pheasants too, and I'd ruined it all.

I found two hens tucked into the wet and muddy grass just a few feet away from where they had escaped. I made a trail of food for them and waited. Mr. Epple carried in a bird. It was easy for him. He knew what he was doing.

When I took off my coat, a gust of flying wind took

away the air in front of me so that just for a second when I inhaled there was nothing there to take in. Holding my coat open, I crept quietly up on the sitting bird. Just as I started to close my coat carefully around her, Mr. Epple was there and he scooped her up with his crooked-fingered hands, tucked her in, smiled big at me, and headed to the pen.

What struck me then as he carried the bird so carefully and gently was how he used to be a boxer. It wasn't just his face and his hands, but the way he stood. He always looked like he was ready for something. Stance. I think that's what it's called.

I waded through an icy mud puddle and got the second pheasant. I held her loosely in my coat and she flapped out of it somewhere close enough to the pen. Mr. Epple and I steered her in.

And then we had nine.

My gut was sick and my mouth all acid.

Mr. Epple laid out more feed and headed back toward the brush, and that's when I chased after him. "Mr. Epple! Mr. Epple! They're not there." I touched his elbow and he turned to face me. "They're not there."

"Don't give up yet," he shouted.

"It's my fault."

He nodded, because it was the most obvious thing in the world and it was obvious that he already knew it. But he thought I was talking about the unsecured pen and the escaped birds. He didn't know what I'd done.

Whipping off my gloves, I showed him the scratches on my wrist. "Last night after the game I came back out here and took two birds."

He looked at my hands and then he nodded and shook his head all at once and then he looked at me.

"I'm sorry. I'm sorry and it was wrong. I thought—I thought—I thought it was the right thing to do."

He shook his head at that.

Dylan said I should write Mr. Epple a note if I had a lot to explain. I don't know what I would have written if I'd had paper and a pencil. I didn't have a clue. "I'll pay you back. I'll pay you for the birds. I'm sorry. It was stupid and I thought it was going to help me. I thought it would solve something." A gift. An egg. A bird. It made me think about my mom and how she sees the big stuff in the small stuff. How small things can get big. How after the tornado when I couldn't believe the school's missing cafeteria hadn't made the news and how she said the small stuff still matters.

How little things add up to big things and multiply. Like saying hi to Homer. Sticking up for him.

Or like knocking on Sydney's door. After.

Or how I hadn't done either.

Mr. Epple waved his arm again and turned and walked away. He wasn't even going to look at me.

"Go," he told me, turning back, swinging his arm out, at the road, at the wide open fields, at the gray sky.

He pointed to his truck. The ride home was as quiet as the ride out—just road noises. It was a loud quiet. It was all there was, all I could hear. It was everything.

CHAPTER 23

MONDAY MORNING I was greeted like the high school quarterback after crushing a rival. Nate ran up to me as soon as I stepped off the bus. He'd been waiting by the bike rack, but it was too cold to ride to school. My bike was wrecked, anyway, all its gears frozen up. I'd have to figure what to do, maybe wash it and grease it up again, because last night I'd stuck all my money in an envelope for Mr. Epple and put it in the mailbox and I wasn't going to get a new bike anytime soon.

Nate pulled me aside and high-fived me and banged both his fists against mine. "Itch! Itch! Oh, man, it's so awesome! I can't believe it, man!" He looked as happy as I'd ever seen him, and that included the time he climbed a tree over the river, jumped in, and then crawled up the muddy riverbank. And the time last year in gym class when we were playing baseball and he pounded a home run so far that we couldn't even find the ball again before the period was over. "You should have told me. I told you I would have helped, but you always told me how hard it would be. I mean, sure, I was hoping." He shook his head. "Let's just say I'm impressed."

Everybody else was there too. Daniel held up a fist for a greeting. "So cool, man."

"Yeah, I'm impressed, Itch," Tyler said, pushing his OSU ball cap up off his eyes. "You actually pulled it off."

Daniel said, "They'd just dropped me off, you know. I can't believe it. Missed the bird on the bus. Highlight of the night."

"Really?" That was Homer, his hands fists on the straps of his backpack. "That was the highlight of the whole night?"

No one paid any attention to him. They bumped all around me, talking, and they bumped Homer right out.

"It was bananas," Sydney said. "A bird on a bus."

Tyler wanted to know if it flew into the windows. He looked unimpressed when Sydney told him it had mostly hunkered down on a cooler but cheered up when Homer told him it had pooped all over. "Had to scrub it off when we got home."

I asked, "Is it okay?"

"Sure," Nate answered. He really was happy. Just, happy. There wasn't a better word for it. "Got to admit, I was worried about you getting me an egg. I know you said it would be the easiest thing, but it would have been real high-risk at my end." He shook his head. "All the same, I never thought you'd be able to pull it off. An actual bird. Didn't think you'd even try. Couldn't believe it when Homeschool called me up Saturday night. Mind. Blown. Found the thing tucked down on the cushion of my chair."

Once, Mrs. Anderson gave a pop quiz with all sorts of crazy instructions on it. "Read carefully," she told us as she passed them out. The instructions were things like *Stand up on your desk. Take off your shoes. Shout your name. Write one thousand and one words explaining the meaning of life.* Some kids started doing the stuff even though they knew it was weird. When Tyler stood up on his desk he stayed crouched down. I didn't do it. Neither did Homer. Nate took off his shoes and warned everyone his feet stank. At the top of the page it said, *Read the entire test before responding.* At the bottom it read, *Do not answer any questions. Write your name at the top of the test and turn the test in to your teacher.* That day I'd gotten it right. Not this time, though. That's what it felt like. How everybody but me was happy.

Tyler asked, "What are you going to do with them?"

"Raise them," answered Nate. "Hopefully she'll lay some eggs."

"Was she okay all night?" That was Homer.

Nate shot him a look and Daniel snickered. "I guess.

Me and my grandpa moved them to an old doghouse at our place."

Daniel said, "What Homer really wants to know is if you had a night-light for the pheasant. Like the one he's got at home."

I said, "You can't keep the bird in a *doghouse*."

Nate shrugged. "Sure you can. We fenced it up. Built a little run for them yesterday. It's better than the storage unit. That's all inside."

"Okay." Maybe it would be better. It would probably be better. I was glad Nate was taking care of it and that the bird hadn't been stressed out all night in darkness.

"My grandma says I can build the birds a real pen in the spring. Hey, Itch, you want to help me with that?"

"Wait, what? What do you mean, *birds*? What *them*?"

"Didn't you hear? Yesterday I was out at the unit and heard these bird noises down the road and do you know what I found? Another pheasant! A rooster! Just, out in the fields! Can you believe it? A wild pheasant when all the wild pheasants are supposed to be gone. Or at least so gone you don't see them walking down the road." He took a breath. "So I got that one too."

Homer looked at me. Nate might think it was a miracle, a ring-necked pheasant strutting down the road, but Homer knew better. "You were trying to save more than one," he said. "Saving birds while we were eating brats and watching the game."

I didn't care what Homer thought. At that moment, I only cared about one thing in the whole world. "How did you get that pheasant, Nate?"

"Like this," he said, shoving his hands in my face. They were covered in red lines. Some of the lines were just scratches and some were deep, like punctures, and he had bandages covering up a couple. Things looked pink around the edges. It looked like he'd been in a wrestling match with the rooster.

"You should have worn gloves."

"Thanks, Sherlock."

"Didn't you see the towel I left behind? You could have used that. Maybe wrap the bird up—"

"I didn't know I was going to get a bird. It was a gift from the universe."

"You washed those cuts, right, Nate?"

"Itch, man, you're starting to sound like Homer now."

"Seriously, Nate. They could get infected. Some of them look kind of ugly already."

Another bus unloaded and kids bumped around us. Everybody else was going inside. It was cold. I could see my breath. Daniel's buzzed and uncovered head was pink and his ears were red. I didn't know how he could stand it.

Everybody started talking about names for Nate's pheasants. Sydney said, "I like Scarlet and Gray."

Daniel said that was no good. "The one with all the colors is the guy and Scarlet is a girl's name and you can't name *him* Scarlet."

"How about Gray and Gray? That sounds kind of cool to me."

"That's just stupid," Nate said.

Daniel suggested using old coaches' names and giving one bird a coach's first name and the other bird the same coach's last name. "Urban and Meyer. Jim and Tressel." Tyler suggested Earle and Bruce and Woody and Hayes.

"Those are all lousy names for the girl pheasant," Sydney said.

Tyler said Tressel wasn't so bad.

"I got it," Homer said. "Urban and Rural."

Conversation stopped dead. The boys made faces at him. "Lame."

"So stupid."

"Sheesh, Homer."

"Of course that's what Homeschool Homer would come up with. How about we name one Foot and the other Ball?"

I didn't think the joke was that bad. Obvious, maybe. And maybe the kind of joke the coach would have heard his whole life, but the way the guys reacted you would have thought Homer had suggested naming the birds for a Michigan coach.

The warning bell rang. We started toward the doors. Homer walked alongside me. "You did it, Itch. You're lucky."

"Okay." It didn't feel that way to me. It was like a math problem when you got the first part wrong and you just got more wrong answers all the way down.

Guess Homer didn't think I was appreciative enough of my new status because he grabbed a strap hanging off my backpack and stopped me short. "Do you know how lucky you are? Everybody's impressed. You're back on the team. You've got a second chance."

"I hate to burst your bubble, but maybe second chances aren't all they're cracked up to be."

"Says you. I'd take a second chance over osmosis any day."

The final bell rang. Homer just stood there. Even though this was Homer's first year in school, I knew he'd never been late for anything ever before and being late would be serious for him. If we made a run for it we might make it. Everybody else had cleared out. Except he still stood there, scowling at me, his hands so tight they were nothing but knuckles.

The sky was a pure blue and it didn't matter that the sun was bright because it hadn't warmed up anything yet.

There were no clouds, only the thin white lines left by airplanes that traced a path through the sky and then floated apart. My mom was on one of those planes. Somewhere. Not over Ohio. She wasn't even going to fly over Ohio, but she was up in the air right now someplace farther west than here—flying over mountains, Dad had said, and over another country still right until the very end, and from up above nothing would look familiar to her yet.

"Homer." I was thinking. Trying to restart. Trying to reboot. "Connor."

He jumped a little when I said his name.

"Don't bother trying anything now," he said. "You got the birds. You're a sixth-grade hero. Don't worry. I won't try to get you to join my team anymore. And you're better off if you stick to calling me Homer."

Remember the note I'd written Sydney and folded into a paper triangle that had been flicked away?

I had it.

I'd picked it up off the floor when I'd left the classroom, itching.

It had hung around in the front pocket of my backpack, but when I was getting ready for school I had to switch to one of my dad's old backpacks because mine was busted and gross with bird feathers and bird smell. Even though I knew right away what it was, I unfolded it. *Sorry.* Sorry is one of those words that kind of says everything but at the same time doesn't say enough.

I'd refolded the note along the lines. It took me a few times to get it right. It was like folding a map, which always seemed like it should be easy but never was.

It rode in my pocket all day.

Because I didn't know. I didn't know if Sydney would ever want to be my friend again. She'd talked to me on the Buckeye Bus, but since it was hard to ignore someone when you're trapped with them and a pheasant, I didn't know if that counted. And this morning. Had she said anything to me? She hadn't said anything to me.

I gave her the note at lunchtime.

First, though, I ran into Mrs. Anderson in the hallway on my way to the gym, and she gave me a big smile and a double thumbs-up. "Stop by my desk after lunch," she told me, looking so happy that it caught me off guard. It had to be my math test. I must have done okay. I must have done better than okay, because she wouldn't smile like that otherwise. "I think you'll be pleased."

Lunch was in the gym and the gym was mostly empty because the PTA had started selling pizza in the lobby on Mondays and everybody was standing in line to buy some. So it was me and Sydney and a handful of other kids. Abby sat up high against the gym wall with Lucas, eating a frozen tube of yogurt and a sandwich. Sydney wasn't going to eat pizza and I wasn't going to eat it either, because it was the gas station pizza.

Sydney unfolded the triangle and held it up. You could tell it was an old note. Worn. Ripped, even though I'd only unfolded and refolded it that once. "What can I say. I've been sorry for a long time. Can I eat lunch with you?"

She folded the note back up but into squares and nodded. "Okay."

"For real?"

"For real." She opened her lunch box and set it up across her knees. She had crackers, lunch meat that she wrapped around carrot sticks before she ate them, a container of black bean dip, a box of chocolate soy milk, and a giant homemade oatmeal cookie.

I sat down next to her. Not right next to her. But next to her. Sydney looked at my lunch. "Is that a tuna sandwich?" she asked.

"Do you think it looks like cat food?"

"Ugh, yes. Get it away from me." She stuck a carrot in the dip. "You could eat the pizza, you know."

"No thanks."

"You know it's bad because it's from the gas station, right? It's not bad because it's cut into squares. Because how the pizza is cut doesn't really affect the taste. I've never eaten that pizza. I only eat homemade. But I still know I'm right."

I pointed to the note next to her on the bleachers. "I mean it," I said. "I am sorry. You know it was a mistake, right? I didn't know what the ingredients were. And, and, I hated it. Seeing you like that."

Sydney made a sound somewhere between a laugh and a snort. "Yeah, I hated it too. More than you."

"Yeah."

We were quiet for a little while. Then Sydney said, "You didn't come to see me. How come you didn't come to see me? I wanted you to come and see me. And then you ignored me. It hurt me that you acted like it never happened."

That feeling where every heartbeat felt like a punch was back. "I was scared."

"Me too. It would have been good to see you."

"I wanted to," I told her, "but I just couldn't. Because it was my fault. I'm really sorry."

"You were my friend. And then you wouldn't even talk to me."

"I didn't mean not to talk to you. I was so upset. And then I got stuck. That day in the gym I froze up."

Sydney was quiet for a moment, and then she said, "Let's go back to being normal. Let's be friends again."

"Is it because I got the pheasant?" Because I didn't want it to be because of the pheasant.

"It's because you're here."

"You sure?"

"I'm sure." She bumped my shoulder.

There was nothing to do then but eat our lunches. My tuna sandwich was okay as long as I didn't look at it or think about cats. Sydney had moved on to her oatmeal cookie. It was about the size of my sandwich. I was jealous. After a while, Sydney said, "Homer sure thinks you're a rock star now."

That made me choke on a laugh. "He doesn't. He's mad. I ruined his party."

"How did you ruin his party? Because you weren't there?"

"Hardly." I finished chewing my bite of sandwich. "Because everybody's talking about the pheasants, I guess, and not the Buckeye Bus."

"Like, two interesting things can't happen on the same day?"

"More like if you're Homer and Itch, only one of the interesting things gets to count."

She looked at me. "I hadn't thought of that."

"School's weird," I said.

Sydney laughed and looked around the gym. "Where is he? He's usually here by now. Do you see him?"

"I don't see him." There was something else I wanted to tell her. "It's not like he said, though, how I was doing something good or cool or whatever." I couldn't stop thinking about Mr. Epple and the way he'd turned away from me and the way he'd cut his hand through the air. It was like a knife. And it was for me.

"He can't eat any of the pizza," Sydney said, "so where is he?"

"Standing in line with everybody else."

"That's stupid."

"He's like that today."

"Stupid?"

"Something." I wasn't a sixth-grade hero the way he'd said, but I could do better. Be better.

Maybe everybody else could be better too. I didn't know. I didn't know what Nate or anybody else would do, but I knew what I was going to do.

"I'm not going to call him Homer anymore." I thought about how he'd looked, outside, when it was just the two of us, and I'd called him his name. His real name.

"Yeah?" Sydney asked. "What are you going to call him?"

"Connor."

"Why are you going to do that?"

"Because," I said, "that's his name."

"Oh. Then I'm going to call him Connor too."

"We should go get him. Tell him to sit with us."

"Homer?" Shaking her head, she said, "I mean, Connor?"

"Yeah. He brought his own lunch just like always." The gym was still pretty quiet. No one was playing basketball yet. "He can hang around those guys if he wants to, but he should know he doesn't have to. Do you have a pen?"

I grabbed the square of the note. Unfolding it, I smoothed it out on the bench. Sydney handed me a pen and I wrote neatly and went over the letters until they were a solid black. *Get better, not bitter.* "What do you think?"

"He said that to me back when the soccer team had a five-game losing streak." She pulled her braid over one shoulder. "Do you think it will work? He'll know what it means?"

I thought about second chances and sometimes not knowing what they were or what to do with them. "I think he needs our help. We ought to try."

Abby scooched over to us. Looking over my shoulder, she read my note. "That's Homer. He'll understand. You're speaking his language."

"His name is Connor," Sydney said. Abby nodded. "We're going to go get him."

"Okay," Abby said. "Let me get Lucas." Lucas had already finished his lunch and sat drawing in his notebook. He came down the bleachers two at a time.

"What's up?"

I showed him the note. Lucas said, "Homer told me that when my stuff didn't get picked for the art show."

Abby said, "It's Connor."

Lucas held up his pencil. "Give me a sec," he said, and he drew a cartoon picture of Connor standing on top of the Buckeye Bus. He wrote out *Connor* in bubble letters.

"Cool."

Sydney asked, "Ready, Isaac?"

"Yeah." I nodded.

"Okay," Sydney said, "let's go."

I looked at the crinkly piece of paper in my hands and then up at everybody. "Keep your fingers crossed."

Then we were off through the blue-tiled hallways until the smell of pizza was stronger than the school smell and we could see the line of kids. Connor stood against the wall. He was the only kid in line holding a lunch box. I smiled at Sydney. She smiled back.

ACKNOWLEDGMENTS

Every person and every family dealing with food allergies is different with different needs, and they may handle things differently than the characters in this book. My characters with food allergies are based on my family's experience, and my character with idiopathic angioedema is based on my experience. Thank you for reading about how my characters navigate their world.

To the kids dealing with food allergies or for whom life has added something extra to your plate (pun not intended): you rock. And so do the people who help take care of you.

Special shout-out to all the room parents, parents of my kids' classmates and friends, Girl Scout troop leaders, coaches, and teachers who help keep my kids safe, read food labels, and text me ingredient labels straight from grocery store. Your kindness and awareness has moved me countless times.

Thank you to Peggy Harkins for her thorough and detailed feedback.

Deepest thanks to my agent, Alyssa Eisner Henkin, for guiding Itch (and me) on this journey. It goes (almost) without saying that this story is what it is because of her commitment, encouragement, and advice.

Thanks to the entire team at Holiday House, including Kerry Martin for the jacket design, and especially to my editor Elizabeth Law, who brought insight and a skilled eye to my story. Thanks also to McKenna Nagle for her keen suggestion.

For my daughters: thank you for your joy and interest in what I do. Having my dream come true is even better because I get to share it with you.

And finally, deepest gratitude to my husband, who can, for the record, explain any math problem with great patience and detail. All the root beer in here is for you.

ABOUT THE AUTHOR

Polly Farquhar has a BA from the University at Albany and an MFA in Creative Writing from the Ohio State University. An upstate New York transplant, she lives in the Columbus, Ohio area with her husband and two children. Like Itch, she has idiopathic angioedema and her children manage life-threatening food allergies.